KU-385-532

THE THIRD RAIL

MICHAEL HARVEY

BLOOMSBURY
LONDON · BERLIN · NEW YORK

PERTH & KINROSS COUNCIL	
05624272	
Bertrams	28/04/2010
HAR	£11.99
SCO	

First published in Great Britain 2010

Copyright © 2010 by Michael Harvey

The moral right of the author has been asserted

Bloomsbury Publishing, London, Berlin and New York

36 Soho Square, London, W1D 3QY

A CIP catalogue record for this book
is available from the British Library

ISBN 978 1 4088 0585 5
10 9 8 7 6 5 4 3 2 1

Printed in Great Britain by Clays Ltd, St Ives plc

Mixed Sources
Product group from well-managed
forests and other controlled sources
www.fsc.org Cert no. SGS-COC-2061
FSC © 1996 Forest Stewardship Council

www.bloomsbury.com/michaelharvey

In memory of
MARTHA LYONS SHORTER
1927–2009

Everybody's got plans . . . until they get hit.

—MIKE TYSON

THE ELEVATED

CHAPTER 1

Robles had been on the platform for less than twenty seconds. He leaned against the railing and peered through layered curtains of snow, at the stone faces of apartment buildings crowding close to Chicago's elevated tracks. The row of windows across from him was dark. The street below, quiet. Robles turned back toward the crowd waiting for the train. To his left stood a secretary type, keeping Chicago's winter at bay with a heavy brown coat that ran to her knees. Beside her was a guy barely out of law school, toting a briefcase that was barely out of the box. A clock wound down inside Robles' head. Fifteen more seconds and he needed to move. He gripped the gun in his pocket and walked back toward the entrance to the L platform. A dark-eyed woman was putting on lipstick and standing by the stairs. Her bad luck. He moved closer and snuck a look down the stairwell. No one coming up. More bad luck for her. Robles pulled the gun from his pocket and held it straight in front of him. He focused on the blue pulse beating tiny wings inside the woman's left temple. Then he pulled the trigger, and the woman dropped straight down. Like a puppet with the strings cut, she was all here and there, arms, legs, and a smear of lipstick across her lips and down her chin. She gurgled once or twice and might have even gotten a look at him before the darkness dropped across her eyes. Ten seconds later, Robles was back on the street. He didn't run until he got to the corner and, even then, not too fast. He didn't want to attract attention. More important, he didn't want to get too far ahead of the man he hoped would pursue.

CHAPTER 2

I took the stairs two at a time, slid over the turnstile and out of the L station. A kick of wind hit me fat in the face, and snow fell sideways as I shouldered my way down Southport Avenue. A soft frat boy and his softer girlfriend stood stiff at the corner of Southport and Cornelia, wearing Northwestern and Notre Dame sweatshirts, respectively, and pointing their slack jaws and wide eyes east. Even if I weren't a detective, it wasn't hard to figure which way the shooter had run. I pulled my nine millimeter, held it low by my side, and turned down Cornelia. A half block ahead, a slip of dark fabric disappeared into an alley. I followed, past a run of single-family homes, two- and three-flats, a block from Chicago's Brown Line. At the mouth of the alley, I leaned up against a graystone and took a quick look around the corner. The run of pavement was empty, save for a string of Dumpsters and a rat the size of a cat that, thankfully, took off for points unknown. I slowed my breathing and listened. The wind had fallen off and the cover of new snow deadened everything, including the footsteps of the guy who had just shot a woman on the platform of the Southport L. I crept up to the first Dumpster.

A scuff of powder told me my guy had turned in to a second alley that snaked off the first, running parallel to Cornelia. I pulled my gun up to shoulder height and crept forward again. More footprints in the second alley, headed east. Whoever he was, he had turned the corner and just kept moving. I slipped my gun back into its holster and took off at a run. I had made it a good ten yards before a body flew up from behind and to my left. I sprawled toward the dusting of snow and hard cement underneath. He kept his body weight balanced and center of gravity low. I tried to shift, but he slipped an arm across the back of my neck and ground my head against the pavement. I relaxed for a second, hoping my guy might as well. Then I felt steel pressed against the base of my skull and stopped moving altogether. A gun will do that to you.

"Easy," the man said and backed off the pressure on his forearm a little. The gun stayed where it was. "Turn around."

I turned my head just enough. The shooter wore a black overcoat with black buttons. A fine spray of liquid clung to the hem of his coat. Blood splatter from the woman as she fell. I looked up. He had a black knit hat on. A ski mask covered his face. I took all that in even as my brain processed the final piece of the puzzle, the dark hole of a .40-caliber handgun, sitting six inches from my forehead.

"Ready to die, hero?" He said it more like he was curious than anything else. Really, genuinely interested in my comfort level with impending mortality. I figured anything I might say would just kick off the festivities. So I didn't say anything. Just looked at the mask and tried to fathom the face beyond. He lifted the gun a fraction and began to pull back on the trigger. You might think you can't see that kind of delicate pressure on a trigger. Trust me, when you're up that close and personal, you notice. So he squeezed back, a pound or two of pressure. Then he stopped, lifted the gun another inch or so, and brought it down, fast, heavy, and hard. After that, it was the rush of Chicago asphalt toward my face and darkness.

CHAPTER 3

Robles was two miles and thirty minutes removed from the Southport L stop. He'd changed into an oversize sweatshirt with a Nike logo on the front and black slashes down the sleeves. He had the hood pulled low over his eyes and stared out a window as the number 136 bus pulled onto Lake Shore Drive for its journey downtown. The snow had stopped as quickly as it started, and the winter sun poured cold light over the city. A woman in a Honda Civic cruised close. She had a cell phone cradled to one ear and fussed in the rearview mirror with the corners of her mouth. Robles watched as her front wheel wandered to the edge of her lane and past, brushing close to the side of the bus. His driver laid on the horn. The woman took her eyes off herself, pulled her car straight, and flipped a middle finger toward anyone and everyone who ever rode the CTA. Then she snapped the cell shut and went back to her face.

Robles felt the anger, hot and uncomfortable inside, but tamped it down. He pulled out a street map of Chicago and took a look at the Loop. He knew the block and traced the route with his finger for what seemed like the hundredth time. He liked to run things through his mind. That way, when it came time to act, there'd be no thinking. Just hit the button, play the tape, and follow along.

Robles stood as the bus turned onto Wacker, walked to the back door, and reached for the grab bar overhead. An old lady sat nearby, tapping her foot and cursing softly under her breath. At first, Robles thought the "motherfucker"s were for him; then he realized she was just another nut job riding the CTA. Robles smiled at the old lady and pictured himself cutting her throat. She looked up, tapped her foot again, and called him a cocksucker. At the front of the bus a radio crackled. The driver picked up his two-way and listened, then asked a question Robles couldn't quite make out. Didn't matter. He had a feeling he knew exactly what all the chatter was about and pulled the cord to request a stop.

The bus angled to the curb at Wacker, on the edge of Chicago's Loop. Robles got off and walked south on Wabash to the corner of Lake. The building was four or five stories high, cut rough from blocks of Indiana limestone and black with soot from the big city's breath. He pulled on a pair of gloves and stepped inside the front door. There was no one in the vestibule, just a line of metal mailboxes and a set of wooden stairs, sinking to the right and winding up. Robles took the stairs, two at a time, until he got to the top floor, turned a corner, and walked to the end of a hall that was long, narrow, and smelled like old diapers. There was a small window at the end, letting in a sad trickle of light onto a wooden door with a silver doorknob. The key was taped under a corner of the synthetic orange carpet, just to the left of the door. Robles turned the lock and walked in.

It was a one-room apartment with a single light in the middle of the room and a second door that probably led to a bathroom. Directly in front of him was a set of three more windows. Larger than the one in the hall, they looked south, out over a landscape of smoke and steel. In the foreground was a curve of green girders and the Loop's elevated tracks, wrapping around the corner at Lake and Wabash.

Robles opened one of the windows and leaned into a cold draft circling up from the street. A pigeon hopped onto a ledge below him and stared. Robles ducked his head back inside and drew a shade across each of the windows. Then he walked over to a white sheet, spread out on the floor in the middle of the room. Under the sheet was a gray gun case. Inside the case, a Remington 700 rifle with a Leupold scope and a box of .308 Winchester ammo. Robles took out the weapon and broke it down. A train rumbled by, rattling the windows in their frames and vibrating the boards under his feet. Robles smiled. They hadn't stopped the downtown runs. Even after the thing at Southport. He didn't think they would. No need. Not yet, anyway.

Twenty minutes later, Robles had reassembled the rifle and loaded a five-round magazine. He spread out a floor pad by the windows, cracked the middle shade to half-mast, and opened the window itself eight inches. Four trains had passed since he'd entered the apartment, about one every five minutes. On the sill in front of him was a CTA train schedule. There'd be another in a minute and a half. Robles slipped the barrel out the window and looked through the scope. It was blurry, so he adjusted, using a billboard asking Chicago to support their Bulls as a marker. Derrick Rose's face popped up in the sight. Another adjustment, and Chicago's savior sharpened into focus. Robles heard a rumble as a train approached the curve of track. His train. Right on time. Robles slipped his finger onto the trigger and leaned into the rifle stock. Then he pulled his head back and listened. The scratching at the door was

soft, but close and very much there. He waited, hoped whoever it was might go away. The knocking, however, persisted,
grew louder, and Robles knew it was fated to be so.

He placed the gun back in its case and covered it over with
the sheet. Then he closed the shade, slipped off his gloves, and
opened the door just as the train rushed by. On the other side
was an old face, hammered down between two shoulders and
pinched with anger at a life that had somehow wound up here.
Robles cared not a bit for any of that. The face was in the way.
The face needed to go away.

"Sorry," Robles said. "I was in the can. You need something?"

"Name's Jim Halter. I manage the place."

Halter's smile revealed a row of large teeth that looked like
unwashed elbows. His eyes were black and busy, slipping over
the threshold and into the room, hungry for whatever there
was to be had: a young girl, a stash of drugs, maybe a whiff of
cash. Robles angled his body to give the building's manager a
better look.

"Nice to meet you, Jim. You want to come in for a second?"

Halter raised a long, veined hand to his face. The nails were
calcified, the skin, spotted.

"No, no," Halter said as he stepped across the threshold. "I
just wanted to check in. Make sure you got settled okay."

"Sure." Robles swung the door shut.

Halter took a quick look behind him and might have been a
little spooked. Then he noticed the white sheet in the middle
of the room. The slippery eyes widened a bit more and a
tongue moistened lips the color of liver.

"The e-mail said you'd be in today," Halter said. "I was a
little leery of leaving a key. But I guess it worked out all
right."

Robles showed him the key. "Worked out fine. Thanks."

Halter nodded and took a second step into the room. Robles crowded close behind. The manager's Adam's apple rolled in its pocket of flesh, and Robles slid the room key back into his pocket.

"What sort of business you in, sir? If you don't mind me asking, that is?"

Halter created space as he spoke, fluttering, like an old and desiccated moth, to whatever sliver of flame lay underneath that magic sheet. Robles let him drift, fitting a six-inch hunting knife to his hand and feeling a familiar hole at the back of his throat. Wet work, Nelson called it. Robles took a calming breath. Wet work it would be.

"Reason I ask," Halter said, "I have a lot of expertise. Connections in the area."

"You do?"

"Sure." The manager began to turn back toward Robles, eager to strike his bargain. Eager to discover what lay hidden. Eager for his piece.

The manager made it, maybe, halfway. Robles grabbed him under the chin and stretched his neck. The cut was clean. Halter collapsed in a rush of air, the wound making a sucking sound like he was trying to breathe through his throat. Robles stepped back. The manager slipped the rest of the way to the floor and lay there, wet, red, and shivering. A soft moan followed and a roll of eyes across the room.

"Shit." Robles took another step back. Halter was bleeding hard, the body in spasm, but well on its way to dead. Robles used the sheet to cover him over. Within a minute or so, the shivering had stopped and the white cotton ran crimson. Robles wiped his blade clean on the sheet and took a quick inventory. He had a smear of blood on his pants and some on his shoes. He cleaned them as best he could. Then he wiped down the doorknob and door. It would have to do.

Robles checked his watch. The whole thing had taken less than five minutes. Not a problem. He slipped his gloves back on, picked up the rifle, and headed back to the windows. He arranged the floor pad again and sat, weapon cradled in his lap. Then he closed his eyes and waited for his pulse to slow. After a minute or so, he opened his eyes, took a deep breath and exhaled. He felt good again, back in the moment. Robles raised the middle shade and reseated the rifle so the barrel was sticking three inches outside the window. He'd been half expecting something like Halter and was glad it was over. Now he fixed his eye again to the scope, scanned the tracks, and waited.

It wasn't more than twenty seconds before a silver L train chugged around the curve and stopped, waiting for a signal to enter the State/Lake station. Robles took half a breath and curled his finger around the trigger. The scope found a middle-aged woman, pale skin and dishwater for eyes, talking on her cell phone and looking at the street below. Next window down was a white kid, greedy mouth and greasy fingers, whole-hogging from a bag of fast food. Robles moved up to the front of the train and lensed the driver, thick-featured and black, staring straight ahead at nothing but two more decades of riding the rails. For any of the three, a pull of the trigger might even be a blessing. God bless America.

The train jolted and started to move again, just slow enough so it was perfect. Robles ran his rifle down the length of the first car, then the second. The process was a real mind fuck. The selection process, who lived and who died. Then the rifle stopped. She was tucked in, toward the back of the second car. Maybe two windows from the back. He sharpened his sights and tracked her as she floated by. A young woman, Latino, with dark hair and cinnamon skin, head bent at a delicate angle, reading something, probably a book she held in her lap. She glowed in the scope, a bloom of light forming around the curve of her skull and playing across the highlights of her features. She looked up, right at him, and he saw a flash of white teeth. Perfect.

He squeezed down on the shutter in his mind, captured the perfect image, even as he squeezed back on the trigger. The pull was clean, sharp, precise. He fired once to make sure the glass shattered, worked the bolt action, and fired again, a second later. Just in case there was anything left alive behind the glass. He didn't see the woman's head explode. Didn't have time. Five seconds after firing, the rifle was tucked back in from the window, shade drawn tight. Thirty seconds later, the weapon was packed away. Then, he was out of the apartment and down the hallway. Robles exited by a basement door into an alley and slipped the rifle case into a Dumpster. He walked to the other end of the alley and stepped into the flow of people on Wacker. At the Merchandise Mart he caught the last Brown Line train before they suspended service for the day.

On his way out of the Loop, Robles could see the conga dance of flashing lights from cop cars, ambulances, and fire engines, fighting their way to help a woman for whom there was no such thing. From his perch atop the elevated, he could just make out a couple of cameramen checking their gear and the first mast being raised from a television live truck. For the third time that day, Robles smiled. Then he settled back into his seat and looked out over the rooftops as his train clattered north.

CHAPTER 4

I had just finished giving my statement when a silver Crown Vic rolled up and Vince Rodriguez got out.

"Heard your name on the scanner. Figured there were maybe a couple hundred Michael Kellys in Chicago. Still . . ."

"Here I am."

"Here you are. You done with them?" Rodriguez nodded toward the half dozen uniforms and forensics working both alleys off Cornelia.

"Yeah. I told 'em they won't find much. Footprints. That's about it."

The detective took a few steps down the alley and found a seat on the back steps of a three-flat. He'd been in Homicide now for almost four years and carried the weight in his shoulders, the dry sorrow in his face. I sat down beside him.

"So tell me," he said.

"What do you want to know?"

"I assume you didn't get a look at the guy."

I shook my head. "I was waiting for the train. It was crowded, thirty, maybe forty people. I heard the pop, saw the lady fall, and took off after him."

"Him?"

"Yeah, it was a him. Black overcoat, black knit hat. Maybe five-ten, medium build. Followed him down Cornelia."

"And you saw him run down here?"

"I saw the back of his coat. Came down the alley and tracked the footprints."

Rodriguez frowned. "How long had it been snowing?"

I shrugged. "Less than ten minutes."

"And his were the only prints?"

I nodded.

"This all in your statement?"

"Yeah."

"Okay, go ahead."

"So I follow the prints, around the corner to the second alley."

"And?"

"And they continue. One set of prints headed straight east. So I take off after them. He jumps me about halfway down. Came out from behind a Dumpster."

"So the prints continue on." Rodriguez walked two fingers across the space between us. "But this guy somehow doesn't?"

"That's right. He's got a ski mask on now and we wrestle a little. Fucker is strong, by the way. Then he pulls out a gun. Black, looked like a forty-caliber."

"Big boy. Did he say anything?"

"Told me to relax."

"That's it?"

"Asked me if I wanted to be a hero."

Rodriguez chuckled. "He doesn't know you too well, does he? I could have told him you live for that hero shit."

"Funny motherfucker you are."

"Then what?"

"Then he pulls back on the trigger. Slow, like he's thinking about it."

"Must have been a nice moment."

"Yeah, well, he stops. Lifts up the gun and just pops me with the butt. I woke up looking up at the snow falling on my face."

"And that's it?"

"That's it. How's the woman?"

"You saw the gun. How do you think?"

"Dead."

"Oh, yeah. Quite a mess over there, and I'm not just talking about our victim."

"The passengers?"

Rodriguez nodded. "This ain't the West Side, Kelly. These people got jobs, money, families."

"West Side don't have families, huh?"

"You know what I mean. These people count. They ain't used to this. Hell, I already got three camera crews set up on Southport. Now let me ask you something about this alley . . ."

Rodriguez's cell beeped. He flipped it open, held up a finger, and walked away. An EMT came over and asked me if I wanted a couple of Advil for my head. I declined.

"You want, we can take you down to Cook County," she said.

"No, thanks," I said. "I like breathing air just fine."

Rodriguez snapped his phone shut and made his way over. "Shit."

"What is it?"

The detective rubbed a hand over his face and looked around for an answer.

"What is it, Rodriguez?"

"We got another one."

"Another what?"

"Another shooting on the L. Goddamnit. Listen, I have to go down there. You gave your statement, right?"

"Yeah."

"All right. Stay on your cell and I'll call you. There's something about this alley we need to figure out."

"Why don't I come with?"

"Why don't you fuck off, Kelly. I'll give you a call."

Then Rodriguez was gone. I wandered back to the medic and her aspirin.

"You know what," I said, "maybe I am getting a little bit of a headache."

"Let me get you those Advil."

We both walked over to the ambulance. She climbed into the back, shuffled through her kit, and came up with a handful of pills. I sat in the front, switched on her scanner, and came up with an address for the second shooting.

"Here you go, Mr. Kelly."

I downed the pills she gave me and scribbled the address on the envelope they came in.

"Thanks," I said. "Feeling better already."

She smiled. I walked a block and a half and hailed a cab. All things considered, the L didn't seem like such a great idea today.

CHAPTER 5

I slouched against a rusted girder Nelson Algren would have been proud of, about a block from the corner of Lake and Wabash. I could see the train up on the tracks, a forensic team working on the hole where a window used to be. There was a traffic jam of cop cars and firemen below, mingling with an avalanche of media. Already most of the details had hit the radio. The local folks might not be geniuses, but it didn't take a genius to connect Southport to the Loop and come up with one hell of a story. On the cab ride down, I listened as a jock named Jake Hartford took calls, opinions on everything from who the serial killer might be to why the city had already dropped the ball. All of this delivered in the highest decibel, the black-and-white shrieks of daytime talk, opinion delivered without any obvious facts or apparent need for them. Up on the tracks, I could see the smudgy outline of Rodriguez, talking to another detective and looking down at the mob on the street. I couldn't see Rodriguez sweat, but I could feel it. After a minute, he took a call. Now I couldn't hear him swear, but I could feel that even more. He snapped the phone shut and searched the rafters of the elevated for some guidance. Then he walked back to the first detective, whispered in his ear, and headed down to the street. I headed that way as well. We met in front of Gold Coast Dogs, with about a dozen reporters and a half dozen cameras between us.

"Detective, do you have any leads on either of the shootings?" The question came from a breathless blonde Channel 10 had hired about a month and a half ago. She probably hailed from somewhere in North Dakota and had never ridden an L train in her life. Still, she was easy to look at. In local news, that counted for a lot.

"We're working both crimes scenes, collecting evidence, taking statements. We should know a lot more once that process is completed."

Rodriguez's cop voice was in full throat, deep and measured. He never made eye contact with the horde. Just looked beyond the cameras, probably wondering why he ever got out of bed in the morning.

"Detective Rodriguez, are you working both cases together or are these separate investigations?"

That was John Donovan, Chicago's senior crime reporter. He was the lead dog, and the rest of the pack knew it. So did Rodriguez.

"We have separate teams working each case. There will, however, be some overlap."

"Meaning you, or some other detective, will be working both cases?" Donovan said.

Rodriguez nodded. "Probably."

"Which means you suspect the two shootings are connected?" Donovan said.

"We don't know what to suspect at this point," Rodriguez

said, voice rising as the media began to write their own story. "There are significant differences in these two crime scenes. Given the circumstances of the shootings, however, we'll certainly be looking into any possible connections."

"Have you got any concrete evidence the two are connected?"

That was from an olive-skinned woman with a notebook and pencil, standing at the back of the crowd, just in front of me. She was slight, maybe thirty years old, with glasses that had slipped halfway down her nose and a look of intelligence you don't often see in a gathering of the media.

"No, we don't have anything specific that connects the two," Rodriguez said. "But, as I indicated, we're in the early stages."

Several reporters jumped in, yelling questions, one over the other. It was Donovan who broke through the maelstrom.

"Detective, does Chicago have a spree killer loose in its public transportation system?"

Rodriguez paused, eyes searching, then resting on me. I could see a small, sad smile flicker at the corner of his mouth. Then he looked at Donovan and offered up the sound bite everyone was waiting on.

"John, I'll be honest. At this stage, we don't know what we're dealing with. Rest assured, however, the entire weight of the Chicago Police Department will be brought to bear on these cases, and we will get some answers."

"When?" Donovan said.

"Soon, John. Sooner rather than later. That much, I can promise you."

With that, Rodriguez ended the press conference. Several people continued to yell questions, but the detective waved them off. After a few minutes, the crowd began to dissolve. The print reporters went back to reporting. The TV folks shot pictures and put on makeup.

RODRIGUEZ DRIFTED ACROSS Wabash and met me at the corner of Randolph.

"Let's get a coffee," he said.

I nodded and we walked back across the street.

"Why am I not surprised you're here?"

I shrugged. "What did you expect?"

"Exactly. What do you think?"

"About what?" I said.

"The press."

"Hysterical, as usual. Maybe even more so."

"This is going to be a fucking zoo."

"You got that right."

We walked into a Starbucks and ordered. Then we sat by the window and looked out at the street.

"You got one shooter here, Vince."

Rodriguez stared me down over his cup of coffee. "You sure about that?"

"Seems logical to me."

The detective took a sip. "One's a walk-up with a handgun. The other, a sniper with a rifle."

"You thinking they're not connected?"

Rodriguez shook his head. "I didn't say that. Just doesn't fit the normal pattern."

I shrugged. "It's the same guy."

"Or guys," Rodriguez said. "Let's talk about your alley."

The detective placed a napkin between us and sketched out

the scene at Cornelia. "You turn the corner here and see a set of footprints tracking all the way down this alley. Right?"

I nodded.

"Okay, the snow had been falling ten minutes. Correct?"

"Tops," I said.

"And there's just one set of prints?"

"Just the one."

"But when you follow the prints, the guy is waiting for you. Halfway down the alley, behind a Dumpster."

"Maybe he doubled back?" I said.

"There'd be two sets of footprints."

"Not if he walked back in his own tracks."

"What is he, Daniel fucking Boone?"

"What are you saying, Detective?"

"What I'm saying is this guy, your shooter, runs down the alley and around the corner." Rodriguez drew a line with an arrow tracing the route. "But a second guy was working with him. Waiting behind the Dumpster."

"To ambush me?"

"Exactly."

I shook my head. "The guy that put the gun on me was the Southport shooter."

"You can't be sure."

"He had blood splatter on his coat. Gotta be the shooter."

Rodriguez studied his drawing for a moment. "Okay, how about this? Second guy is set up in the alley. He sees our shooter take the corner and starts running."

"And the shooter takes the second guy's place behind the Dumpster," I said. "That's how it went down. Had to be."

"Maybe," Rodriguez said. "But here's the ballbreaker . . ."

"Why?"

"Exactly. Why would our shooter have an accomplice waiting in the alley, for you or anyone else, to come by? Unless that was the point of the whole exercise, the reason they shot up the station at Southport in the first place."

"If I was the target, why not shoot me in the head when you have the chance? Why let me go? Doesn't make sense."

Rodriguez sighed and threw his coffee cup into a barrel. "Since when do assholes like this make sense?"

I was about to respond when my cell phone buzzed. I picked up and found some answers at the other end of the line. Not to mention someone I like to think of as a grade-A asshole.

CHAPTER 6

Nelson held the cell phone tight to his ear, looked across the street, and through Starbucks' front window.

"Michael Kelly, how are you?"

"Do I know you?" Kelly's voice was gruff and aggressive. Certain, but curious. Pure cop, even if the man himself was no more.

"Do you know me? I believe I put a gun to your head earlier this morning. A lot of fun that. Then I picked up a Remington 700 with a scope and blew the brains out of one of Chicago's many drones on the CTA. If you want to check my bona fides, that is."

The silhouette in Starbucks raised his chin and gestured to the cop sitting next to him. Nelson smiled.

"Tell Detective Rodriguez, the bullet's a Nosler AccuBond, one-eighty grain, loaded into a Black Hills .308 Winchester. Specially designed to fire through glass. By the way, how's the coffee there? Starbucks is a piece of shit in my book. Then again, I heard they're grinding their own beans. Getting back to basics. I like that."

Kelly had to be surprised he was being watched. Still, the man's head didn't move.

"You didn't look around. Very good, Kelly. You'd never see me anyway. And don't worry. I have my eye on you, but not through the scope of a weapon. That's long gone, so tell Chicago's finest not to look too hard for it."

"What do you want?"

"What do I want?" Nelson snorted into the cell. "I don't want you dead. Could have checked that off the to-do list today. No, you're going to suffer a little bit first. A matter of honor, I think."

"What would you know about honor?"

"Homer pegged it as a zero-sum game. The more you suffer, the greater my glory."

Kelly's silhouette seemed to stiffen at the classical reference. "You're gonna die, asshole."

"Undoubtedly. The question is: How many am I taking into the hole with me?"

Nelson cut the line and waited. Kelly flipped his phone shut and leaned across to the detective named Rodriguez. Nelson could see them talking. Then the detective reached for a radio and held it close to his lips. Nelson unplugged the adapter he'd used to alter his voice. He tossed his cell phone into the Dumpster he was crouched behind and stripped off the skin-color gloves he had on. Then he pulled out a shopping cart filled with old cans and newspapers and began to push it down the alley. Somewhere a church bell struck twelve. The old man picked up his pace. If he hustled, he could still make the 12:30 mass.

CHAPTER 7

I watched as a woman standing ten feet away ordered a skim mocha, no whip. Rodriguez was whispering into his radio, telling someone somewhere that the killer, or maybe his accomplice, had just given me a ring. The woman was in her early thirties, with light brown hair tied back into a ponytail and a large emerald cat pinned to her dark blue coat. She smiled as the tall, angular barista pushed her drink across the counter. Then the woman took a sip and found her way to a corner table looking out at the street. She pulled out a paperback, tucked one leg underneath her, and began to read. It looked pretty peaceful, pretty nice. I wanted nothing more than to join her. Then Rodriguez got done with his radio machinations and gave me a tap on the shoulder.

"We gotta go."

I knew that was coming. As we exited the Starbucks, four cruisers sealed off the block. Ten cops got out and began to comb alleys, roust bums, and shake down regular folks on the street. I figured too little, too late.

"You got a car?" Rodriguez said.

"No."

"Good." Rodriguez popped the locks on his Crown Vic. "Get in."

Five minutes later, we were out of the Loop and headed west.

"Not going to headquarters?" I said.

The detective shook his head. "Looks like the feds might be taking over. Possible terrorist acts."

"Bet downtown loved that."

"Brass doesn't mind. If it goes well, we'll stick our nose in the trough, suck up as much glory as we can. If we have bodies stacking up on L platforms in a week and a half, we got someone to blame it on."

"Don't you love your job?"

"Funny guy. Right now you're the star of the show."

"Great."

"That's right. Now, talk to me about the guy on the phone. Was he legit?"

"You tell me."

Rodriguez took a left onto Canal. "A patrol found a rifle in the trash. Remington with a scope."

"He told me we wouldn't find it," I said.

"Guess he lied. Try to get over it."

"How about ammo?"

Rodriguez took a right and accelerated down the block. "We'll know more when we pull the lead out of our victim. But there were three rounds in the rifle."

"And?"

"Black Hills Gold, .308 Winchester. Just like your boy said."

"This guy wasn't our shooter."

"How do you figure?"

"He knew we were sitting in a Starbucks, which means he was close by, watching."

"So?"

"Who's gonna shoot up an L train, then hang around the scene and call me for kicks?"

"Then he's our accomplice?" Rodriguez said. I shrugged as we came up on a line of traffic stopped at a red light.

"One more thing." Rodriguez looked over. "They found a second body downtown."

"On the train?"

The detective shook his head. "Building on Lake. Building manager got his throat cut. Apartment looks over the tracks."

"So the manager maybe barges in on our shooter?"

"Or the manager was helping him and then became expendable. Either way, we'll process it. Pull any rental records."

"Our guy isn't that stupid."

"Really?" Rodriguez lifted an eyebrow. "If you got all the answers, let me ask you this: Why are these geniuses calling you?"

"Not a clue."

"Might want to do some figuring on that before we sit down with the feds. You can start with how these guys got your cell phone number. And end with why they didn't drop the hammer on you this morning."

"Shit."

"Exactly. Let's get moving here."

Rodriguez flicked on his siren and flashers. The sea of cars parted, and the detective hit the gas.

CHAPTER 8

Nelson rumbled his shopping cart to a stop at the corner of Superior and State and looked up at the white stone of Holy Name Cathedral. The morning had gone as well as he could have hoped. Robles had gotten their attention. Kelly was involved. Now it was time to make them understand why.

Nelson stashed his cart in an alley and trudged up the steps. With the push of a finger, ten tons' worth of bronze door swung open, and he slipped inside. The 12:30 mass was just starting. The regular crowd was there. Maybe fifty people, mostly folks from work who used their lunch hour to pray. Nelson took a seat in the back and looked them over. The standard hypocrites, getting on their knees and groveling when they needed something: a clean X-ray from the doctor, a phone call from an old girlfriend, a pregnancy test with an empty round window. When you got right down to it, there were very few atheists in the foxholes of life. It was something the Catholic church had understood for centuries and counted on.

To his right, Nelson saw a bench full of three bums like

himself, except they were already asleep. The church toler-
ated them as long as they didn't smell too bad or snore too
loud. The service usually ran twenty-five minutes, tops. The
priest was an old one. No surprise there. He was talking about
running through your own personal Rolodex, checking off the
people you've met, places you've been, and things you've
done.

"How does your Rolodex look?" the sanctimonious bastard
croaked, staring down his saintly nose at the great unwashed.
"Does it bear up under scrutiny? Do you have the right balance in your life? The right priorities? Or are you allowing
your time on earth to be bought and sold, bartered away in the
minutiae of the everyday, the pursuit of the material and your
own comfort? Indeed."

The priest let the last flourish hang as he shook his long
head from side to side and tucked his hands inside embroi-
dered robes.

I'll show you some fucking priorities, Nelson thought and
let his eyes wander up to the ceiling. Five galeri hung there,
red hats with wide brims, representing five dead Chicago cardinals. Five princes of the church, more hypocrites presiding
over an empire that was as rotten as it was rich, as calculating
as it was pretentious.

Nelson felt inside an inner pocket for the small brown
bottle. It had a cork stopper in it. He stood up and wandered
into the rear vestibule. A Chicago cop was there, loaded down
with a radio, nightstick, and gun and sweating in a bulletproof
vest. He considered Nelson's filth and turned back toward the
service. Nelson shuffled over to the stone cistern that held the
holy water and waited. Communion was called, and the cop
went forward to get his wafer. Nelson dipped dirty fingers in

the bowl and blessed himself with the magic water. Then he slipped the brown bottle from his jacket and tipped its contents into the bowl.

Communion was over and people were starting to wander to the back of the church. Nelson stepped away from the bowl and watched a mother approach, young child in tow. Nelson smiled. The woman recoiled. Still, she was Catholic and soldiered on, pretending to like the bum and nodding in his direction. She touched her fingers to the water and blessed herself. The young girl beside Mom held her arms up. Before the woman could react, Nelson lifted the girl so she was level with the cistern. He smiled again at the mother as her child sprinkled the water across forehead and cheeks. The mother reached for the child, hustling away once she had the girl back in her arms. Nelson watched them go. Then he crouched in a corner as the rest of the congregation filed out. A couple dozen took holy water. After a bit, the church was empty. Nelson walked outside and shuffled his way to the back of the building. He found his shopping cart, gritted his teeth, and began to push into the wind along State Street.

CHAPTER 9

Rodriguez and I walked into FBI headquarters at a little after noon. A young Asian woman in a blue suit took our names and guns in exchange for plastic IDs. Then she walked us through a door and down a hallway, where she passed us off to a young white man in a brown suit. He put us in a small office and told us someone would be with us shortly. An hour later, the door to the office opened. On the other side was a young black man in a gray suit. He took us another twenty feet to a conference room, filled with all sorts of men and women, clad in all sorts of suits. They all stopped talking as we walked in, and everyone seemed exceptionally good at not smiling.

"This is Detective Vince Rodriguez and, I suspect, Michael Kelly?" The man speaking carried his sixty or so years alarmingly well. His face was largely unlined, his eyes clear, his hair an efficient salt-and-pepper flattop. He cloaked broad shoulders in a custom-cut three-button suit and walked with the natural grace of an athlete. On his left wrist, he wore a gold watch; on his left hand, a wedding ring. He shot his cuffs as he approached, flashing a set of FBI logos disguised as cuff links.

"Dick Rudolph. Deputy director of the FBI."

I shook the deputy director's hand and glanced toward Rodriguez, wondering how and why the FBI's second-in-command happened to be in Chicago, and how and why he didn't have better things to do than talk to me. Rudolph seemed to read my mind.

"I'm in Chicago on some unrelated business, was scheduled to fly out this afternoon, when this thing jumped up. Sit down, Mr. Kelly."

I took a seat beside Rodriguez. Rudolph staked out the head of the table and did his best to make me think I was at least the second-most-important guy in the room.

"As you might imagine," Rudolph said, "the nature of these crimes has sparked concern along several different lines, including possible terrorist acts. The Bureau has stepped in to help, and I decided to sit in on today's meeting."

Rudolph turned to the rest of the table. "Mr. Kelly is a former Chicago police officer. Now, a private investigator. As you all know, he was on the Southport L platform this morning and confronted our suspect in an alley. He also took the call from our suspect. You have copies of his statement and details on the call. We've asked Mr. Kelly to come in and see if he could be of any further help."

His role apparently played, the deputy director sat back and waited. A woman across the table cleared her throat. She was thirty-five, maybe forty, with nervous eyes and a tough mouth that would have been attractive if it wasn't so disapproving. I'd seen it before. Battle fatigue from too many years in the Old Boys' Club.

"Mr. Kelly, my name is Katherine Lawson. I'm heading up our field investigation." Lawson had long, thin hands that she folded in front of her as she spoke. Her fingers were devoid of any jewelry, save a gold ring with a black stone that also carried an FBI crest. I guessed cuff links didn't work for her.

"Did you, by any chance, recognize the man in the alley?" Lawson said.

"He was wearing a ski mask," I said. "It's in my statement."

"Voice?"

I shook my head. "Sounded young. Plenty strong and looked to be in good shape."

Lawson glanced down at her notes. "He asked if you were ready to die?"

"That's right."

"Any idea why he said that?"

I shrugged. "I assume he was just making conversation."

Lawson caught her boss's eye. Rudolph seemed to be watching the exchange closely, but kept quiet.

"And why would you assume that?"

The last question came from a black man with white tufts of hair planted on either side of his head and a trim white goatee. He was sitting at the far end of the table, his chair turned to face the nearest wall.

"This is Dr. James Supple," Lawson said. "He works with our Profiling Section out of Quantico."

I nodded, but Supple continued to study the wall. Fuck him. Fuck profilers.

"He didn't pull the trigger," I said. "What else should I assume?"

Supple turned a fraction in his chair. A smile licked at the corner of his lips. "So the suspect was playing with you?"

"You mean suspects," I said.

Supple sat up a bit. "Excuse me?"

"Suspects," I said. "There were two suspects in that alley. Not at the same time, but they were there."

I went on to explain the theory Rodriguez and I had worked out.

Supple shook his head and glanced at Rudolph. "Doubtful."

"Why?" the deputy director said.

"A killer like this almost always operates alone." Supple plucked his glasses off his nose and wiped them down as he spoke. "I know, everyone cites the DC sniper. But that was a unique set of facts. A man and a boy. Student and teacher. The exception, rather than the rule. I can tell you, without any doubt, this suspect almost certainly works without an accomplice."

If they hadn't taken my gun at the door, I would have considered shooting the profiler where he sat. Instead, I took a sip of bad coffee and worked on summoning my reflective self.

"The phone call you took, Mr. Kelly. About how long did it last?" That was Agent Lawson, dutifully picking up the ball and trying to move it forward.

"Less than a minute."

"And the voice on the phone, was it the same as the voice in the alley?"

"The voice on the phone was disguised. Electronically altered. Must have had some sort of device tapped onto the line."

"And why would he do that, do you suspect?" Supple was back again, laying out his piece of cheese and waiting to pounce. Fuck it. Let him pounce.

"I have no idea," I said. "Why?"

"You had heard his voice once in the alley, and he wanted to make sure you didn't hear it a second time, especially if there was a possibility you might record it."

"Let me guess," I said. "That supports your theory of a single shooter?"

"The facts speak for themselves, Mr. Kelly."

"Really? Because it seems to me if he'd let me hear his voice in the alley, why would he go to the trouble of disguising it the second time around? And why would he think my cell would be set up to record a call I had no reason to suspect I was even receiving?"

Lawson intervened again. "What's your point, Mr. Kelly?"

"My point is pretty simple. This guy disguised his voice because he was afraid I might recognize it. Not from this morning, but from some other time."

"So you think this is someone you know?" Lawson said.

"Like I said, we have two people working together here. The one I met in the alley and had never come into contact with before. And the second, the one who disguised his voice and called me out by name. Even referenced my background in the classics."

Lawson consulted her notes again. "You mean his mention of Homer?"

"That's right."

Supple was shaking his head slowly and chuckling. "Mr. Kelly doesn't understand the pathology of the crime. He suspects himself to be the focus of our killer's attention when, in fact, he's a smoke screen. Our killer does a little research into his background. Easy enough to obtain. Then he plays on the private investigator's ego, draws him into the case to distract us. Meanwhile, the actual target, as we all can see from today's events, is much bigger. The intent, far more subtle."

I was reconsidering the many different ways to render my profiler friend unconscious when the deputy director cleared his throat at the end of the table. "Let's not get ahead of ourselves, people. It's still a bit early in the game to be drawing too many conclusions. Agent Lawson, anything else?"

Lawson took the hint and shrugged. "I think we're good for now."

Rudolph stood up and extended his hand. "Mr. Kelly, thanks for helping out. If you could give us a few moments?"

And then I was gone, out of the inner circle, armed with a new appreciation for why people consider a life of crime to be such a lucrative career choice.

CHAPTER 10

The feds stuck me in another small room, this time with a pot of cold coffee and a door that was locked. Every ten minutes, a sallow-faced woman would check to see if I had accomplished anything worthwhile—like, perhaps, hanging myself. No such luck. After two more hours of nothing, Rodriguez walked in.

"Let's go," he said.

"So soon?"

The detective grimaced and handed me my coat. We didn't say much more until we had cleared the building and were safely in his car.

"They're not happy."

"I wouldn't think so," I said.

"They can't get a handle on any pattern to the shootings. And they definitely don't like the fact that he called you."

"And then there's all those dead people."

Rodriguez ignored me. "They're thinking of giving you a new cell phone, one with your old number. If this guy calls again, they'd be able to trace it. By the way, Rudolph's worried you might go to the press."

"Rudolph's a fucking moron. Not as much of a moron as that profiler, but he's still awfully dumb."

"Yeah, well, the good news is Lawson thought you'd keep your mouth shut, and that seemed to carry a lot of weight. Still, it's the Bureau. They don't trust anyone. Especially, anyone inside."

"Who said I was inside?"

"You're not. So that's another point in your favor. At least, it was."

"What does that mean?"

Rodriguez sighed and spun the wheel. His car scraped onto Halsted Street and accelerated. "Rudolph decided the Bureau doesn't want to be on the hook alone in case they don't catch this guy."

"Let me guess, a task force?"

"Just got off the phone with the mayor and my boss. Local, state, and federal. Lawson is running point."

"Bet the mayor loved that."

"I'm the scapegoat for the city."

"Even better."

"Fuck you, Kelly. At the end of the call, Lawson pipes in that she might want you attached to the investigation."

"As what?"

Rodriguez pulled his car to the curb in front of a fire hydrant at the corner of Halsted and Adams.

"That's what the mayor wanted to know. Come on, let's go."

Rodriguez popped out of the car and walked across the street. We were in the heart of Greektown, home away from home for out-of-town businessmen looking for a shot of ouzo, a leg of lamb, or a wayward belly dancer.

We ducked our heads inside a restaurant called Santorini.

The bar was warm and filled with dark men in starched white shirts with nothing to do. Rodriguez flipped open his badge. The bartender smiled and nodded toward a set of stairs. Rodriguez turned to me.

"He's at a table upstairs, Kelly."

"Who?"

"Who do you think? And don't be an asshole."

I WALKED UP two flights alone and surfaced in a dining room that was as large as it was empty. A burst of sizzle and flame flared to my left. Two small Greek men danced around a table, clapping their hands and crying "Oopah" while a third worked on containing the small inferno he'd created. In the midst of it all, Mayor John J. Wilson sat and scowled. The dish was called saganaki, essentially a piece of cheese doused in booze and set on fire. Wilson had a forkful halfway to his mouth as I approached. The mayor waved me to an empty chair.

"You like this shit, Kelly?"

I shrugged. "It's fried cheese. What's not to like?"

"Give him a piece," Wilson said. The waiter smiled and set another hunk of cheese on fire. After I had my portion, Wilson gave the boys a look, and they disappeared downstairs. We were alone. Just me, the mayor, and our saganaki.

"Feds busting your balls, Kelly?"

"A little bit, yeah."

The mayor pointed his fork my way. "How the fuck is it you're in the middle of this?"

"I don't know."

"Coincidence, huh?"

I shrugged. "Could be."

"You're a liar." Wilson cut off another piece of his appetizer and smiled as he chewed. "But that's okay. Everyone lies."

"You think so?"

"Sure. In a way, all the bullshit lies restore my faith in human nature."

"That's comforting."

"For what it's worth, the feds are trying hard to believe you. The female agent, what's her name?"

"Lawson. Katherine Lawson."

"Right, Lawson. She thinks you have a connection. But she's not sure what it is. Anyway, she wants to keep you close. Keep an eye on you. You gonna eat the rest of that?"

I shook my head. The mayor shoveled my saganaki onto his empty plate and continued talking.

"I come here two, three times a week. Sometimes for lunch. Sometimes just to get the fuck away. Listen to these crazy bastards run around, yell 'Oopah,' and all that shit. Glass of wine. Good fish here. You like fish?"

"Sure."

"Me, too. This is a steak town and I love it. But a good piece of fish is tough to beat. Anyway, the Bureau wants you around, but they don't want you in their way."

"I'm sure you can understand why."

"I certainly can. You're an asshole. Simple as that. Don't give a fuck who you fuck. Or why. Can't be reasoned with, et cetera, et cetera. Don't get me started. I already got some indigestion working. You want dinner?"

"No thanks, Your Honor."

"Yeah, I don't really feel like eating with you, either. So, here it is. The feds are going to use you as their personal piss boy. And you're not going to like that. Not one bit. Am I right?"

"When you put it that way . . ."

"Meanwhile, I got some asshole shooting people on the CTA. No rhyme. No reason. Just for the hell of it. And where the fuck does that stop?"

As he spoke, a flush of crimson rose in the mayor's cheeks, a darker thread of purple pooling in the cracks of his fractured complexion.

"I don't know," I said.

"Me neither." The mayor gestured around the empty dining room. "Look at this place. Two nights ago I was in here, and the joint was packed. A week from now, who knows? People get afraid to come out of their house."

"Or their hotel room."

"Exactly. You know how much tourist money this kind of thing could cost us?" Wilson took a sip of water and cracked hard on the ice in his mouth.

"What do you want from me, Mr. Mayor?"

Wilson chewed up his ice and swung his head around the empty room. "Stand up for a second."

I did. The mayor walked behind me and executed a pretty impressive pat down.

"Don't think you're anything special. These days I check my wife for a wire before we get into bed at night."

"Nice life."

"Yeah, sit down." I did. Wilson leaned forward and let his jaw hang open so I could see his back teeth. "I need you to work this case for me. Under the radar. No official ties to the city."

"Just you and me?"

"And Rodriguez. He'll be my eyes and ears with the feds, who, for my money, are gonna get nothing done with their task force."

"You don't feel good about the Bureau?"

Wilson waved a cold hand in my face. "Fuck them. Bunch of pencil pushers sitting around in meetings trying to figure out the quickest way to get their ass back to Washington. Meanwhile, this guy is out popping people. My people. In my city. Our city, for Chrissakes."

"I know."

"So get on it. If you got an angle to play, go ahead and play it. You don't want to tell me your connection to all of this, fine. I'll provide cover for you. Rodriguez will provide whatever information the task force digs up."

"What do you mean by 'cover,' Your Honor?"

"You know what I mean."

"I'd like to hear it."

Wilson leaned in farther, his voice crawling across the table on its belly. "You want to hear it, Kelly? Fine. Find this guy. Guys. Whatever. Put a bag over his head and drop him down a fucking hole. No arrest. No trial. No questions asked."

"You can't find a cop to do that for you?"

"This isn't a Chicago operation."

"And task forces can get complicated."

"That's right. Let me ask you a question. Can you find this guy?"

"Maybe."

"You have an angle, you cocksucker."

"Maybe."

"And the feds are fucking useless, right?"

I shrugged. "I wouldn't say that. The feds are gonna use their methods, like they always do. Sometimes they work . . ."

"And usually they don't. If you don't want to drop someone down a hole, that's not a problem. Just get a line on him and we're good. I'd offer your badge back, but you're too much of an asshole to accept it, right?"

"Right."

"Okay, then. We'll figure out something else for you. Just find this guy. Now get out of here so I can order dinner."

Sometimes the less said, the better. Every instinct told me this was one of those times. So I left the mayor and his offer floating in the Grecian darkness.

CHAPTER 11

Rodriguez was waiting in the car outside Santorini. "How'd it go?" he said and turned over the engine. "How do you think?"

"So what are you going to do?"

"I'm gonna work it. You already knew that. So did Wilson."

Rodriguez pulled into a line of early evening headlights streaming north on Halsted. "Let me guess, on your own terms?"

I shrugged. "What are the feds focusing on?"

"About what you'd expect. Physical evidence, witness statements. They're developing an offender profile, gonna run all their data through NCIC, VICAP, and every other database they can think of."

"What about the rifle?"

"Preliminary from Ballistics established it as the sniper kill. No prints. They're running a trace right now."

"And the apartment?"

"Should have some information in the morning. By the way, the morning should be a lot of fun. City's putting uniforms on all the CTA platforms. Plainclothes on board the buses."

"That's a lot of manpower."

"It gets better. The Bureau wants to put its own teams up on the rooftops. From Evanston to Ninety-fifth. North, south, east, and west. Along every mile of L track."

"Snipers?"

"Whole nine yards. Balaclava, painted faces, rifles with scopes, all that crap."

"Maybe they'll just scare the shit out of these guys."

"Or the half million people who use the L every day. Wilson didn't like it. Said he wasn't going to turn his city into some unholy fucking vision of Baghdad."

"He'll be changing his tune if another body turns up," I said.

Rodriguez grunted. We slipped across the tip of Goose Island, clattered over Clybourn Avenue, and took a left onto Lincoln.

"What's the story with Lawson?" I said.

Rodriguez chuckled. "Thought you might get to that. They call her Sister Katherine."

"Why's that?"

"You remember Father Mark?"

"Doesn't ring a bell."

"Father Mark was the pastor at St. Cecilia's over on the Southwest Side. Took the parish for a little more than a million dollars over five years."

"Heartwarming."

"Yeah, he was shorting the collection money, using parish credit cards, everything. Lawson was the one who got onto him. Spent six months hip deep in church records looking for loose cash. Turns out this guy had a second home in California and three Beemers. When Lawson grabbed him, he was planning to sell the rectory and buy himself a boat."

"That's her big score?"

"That's what she's known for."

"She a climber?" I said.

"Depends on who you talk to. Some say she's always wanted to be a player in Washington. Just never made the cut."

"And the rest?"

"One agent who's been around awhile told me the exact opposite. Says the woman is right where she wants to be. Says she's got big-time pull downtown, but no one is sure with whom or why." Rodriguez glanced across the car. "Bottom line, this guy says: 'Don't fuck with Katherine. She'll ruin your week.' "

"I'll keep that in mind."

Rodriguez flicked his turn signal, took a right onto Southport Avenue, and pulled to the corner at Eddy.

"Tomorrow?" I said and reached for the door handle.

"Hang on." Rodriguez killed the engine. My hand slipped off the handle, and I pushed back in my seat.

"What is it?"

"You tell me," Rodriguez said.

I tried to hide behind a smile that was too quick for its own good. My friend the detective was having none of it.

"Been two months since you went out to L.A. Haven't seen you. Talked to you. Nobody's seen you, except Rachel."

"People get busy."

"Yeah, well, that's fine. But I still need to know you're okay for this."

"You think L.A.'s gonna keep me from the job?"

"I'm not saying that."

"Then what are you saying." I felt the screws tighten in my voice, the pressure build behind my eyes.

"Your father passed. You went out to L.A. to pick up his ashes and came back empty-handed."

"For a guy who doesn't know much, you're pretty well informed."

"Losing your dad can be rough, Kelly."

"Yeah, he was a real fucking prize."

"I lost mine when I was fourteen."

I'd known Rodriguez for four years, but didn't know that. Never thought to ask.

"I'm sorry to hear that," I said and looked across the car. The detective's face was rutted by memory and his voice grew large in the small space between us.

"He worked the swing shift at U.S. Steel. One night he was coming out of the plant. Had the key in the car door when a squad car hit the corner on two wheels, chasing a kid in a hot box. The kid's car bounced my dad off the side of a Buick. Cracked his head open.

"By the time I got to the ER, the docs had done what they could, which wasn't much. He couldn't talk 'cuz of the tubes, and that was probably just about right. But he took my hand and we sat there, waiting. Didn't take too long, either. Eyes filled up with that look. Fucking head went over. And just that quick, my old man was gone."

Rodriguez snapped his fingers, a dry sound, and shrugged.

"Who wants to cry at fourteen, right? But, goddamn, if I didn't sit down on the floor of that hospital and do exactly that. I didn't know my dad. Never got a good word out of him, or even a kick in the ass. But he was my dad. And I cried. And it was the right thing to do."

Rodriguez was finished then, and we both listened to the weather. There was a storm boiling over the lake, and the wind was rising around us.

"I'm okay for the job," I said and hunted for the hint of desperation in my voice.

Rodriguez nodded. "I believe you. But it's still gonna come. Sooner or later. Just because it's your dad. And that's how that is. Now get the fuck out of here and get some sleep."

I slipped out of the detective's car and watched it roll into the night. Then I walked down Eddy to Lakewood. My building was painted in strips of hard streetlight. The hawk was rattling garbage cans in an alley and banging a wooden sign against the side of a tavern. I bundled myself into a doorway and considered calling it a day. I was tired and wanted nothing more than to crawl into an early bed. Lately, however, there'd been no percentage in sleep.

MY CAR WAS parked a half block from Wrigley Field. The Friendly Confines were dark, save for a red neon scrawl atop the main gate, touting regular season tickets, a bargain at a hundred bucks a pop. I turned the car around and drove west. At a stop sign, I pulled out my cell and punched in a number.

"Mr. Kelly?"

"You ever say hello, Hubert?"

"Hello, Mr. Kelly."

"Call me Michael."

"I'd prefer Mr. Kelly, if that's all right."

"How you doing?"

"Okay."

"You still with the county?"

I had met Hubert Russell at the Cook County Bureau of Land Records. He helped me with some library research on the Chicago fire. Then the twenty-something cyberhacker went virtual to help me catch a killer.

"Nah, I left there a few months ago."

"'Cuz of me?"

"Heck, no. I told you. I wanted out of there, so I left."

"Good. Listen, you got a couple of minutes to talk?"

"Right now?"

"Tomorrow morning."

"Have anything to do with all the stuff going down today?"

"How'd you guess?"

There was a pause. "Where do you want to meet?"

"How about Filter over on Milwaukee? Maybe early? Eight a.m.?"

"See you there."

"And Hubert?"

"Yeah?"

"Bring your laptop."

"No kidding."

"And all the toys."

Hubert Russell laughed. Maybe at me. Maybe not. Then he hung up. I flipped my cell phone shut and steered my car through the night, toward the highway and the sainted Irish of Chicago's South Side.

CHAPTER 12

Nelson closed the red binder he'd been reading from, stood up, and looked out at a million-dollar view of Chicago's skyline. He had found the place by accident—a white ghost of a building on the edge of an orgy of gentrification, the last remnants of the city's Cabrini-Green housing complex, patiently awaiting Mayor Wilson's wrecking ball. The high-rise still had heat, still had electricity, and was forgotten by everyone, save the rats. It was perfect for their time frame. Nelson just had to make sure Robles was careful. So far, so good.

A floorboard creaked, and Nelson turned. His shooter was slouched in the doorway.

"Cable?" Nelson nodded toward the silent TV set up in the corner.

Robles smiled and glided across the room. "Relax, old man. We ain't paying." Robles reached down and turned up the volume. CNN was still carrying wall-to-wall coverage of the shootings. The banner headline read: KILLER ON THE CTA.

"This is so fucking wild." Robles squatted on the floor and stared at the screen. A picture of a young Latino girl flashed up. The caption pegged her as a sniper victim. The girl was smiling. The talking head said her name was Theresa Pasillas. She was a senior at Whitney Young High School and had just been accepted at Stanford. Now she was dead. Already they were laying out the black and marching through the streets of Pilsen, the city's largest Latino neighborhood. Nelson turned down the volume on the set.

"Tell me about today," he said.

"Turn it up and we both can learn about it."

Nelson turned the set off altogether. They had spoken once by phone after the second shooting, but Robles hadn't offered up a lot of detail.

"You didn't tell me about the building manager," Nelson said.

"What about him?"

"The news said he was found inside the apartment."

Robles took a sip from a bottle of water. "Dude came in, started sniffing around. I took him with the knife."

"No anger?"

The smile moved easily across Robles' face. "Knife went in and the old bastard dropped."

"What about Kelly?"

"What about him? I already told you. He tracked your footprints down the alley. I put the gun on him."

"And?"

"And what? Didn't seem to bother him much." Robles pulled out a long knife and pointed it at a locked door on the other side of the room. "She still here?"

"She's here."

"Can I have her?"

"What did I tell you?"

"You said I could have her."

"Later."

Robles drew himself up into a sulk. "I could take her any-time I want."

"I know, but you won't."

Robles flicked a wrist and buried his knife a half inch into the wall. He'd done his first killing for his country—as a Ranger with the Eighty-second Airborne in Mogadishu. Upon his return to the States his taste for blood only deepened, and trouble began to tick. The military knew something was wrong, which would have been okay if they could have turned it to their advantage. But they couldn't. So they hit him with a general discharge. After that, he wandered up and down both coasts. Hunting, Robles liked to call it. By his own count, he'd killed maybe a half dozen women before coming to Chicago. Taken a few kids along the way, as well. Nelson put a stop to all that. He replaced common lust with calculated bloodshed and succeeded where the army had failed, harnessing the violence, molding Robles to suit his purposes. The ex-Ranger was a dangerous, if mostly willing, pupil. And even brought his teacher a very special gift.

"You still got the case I gave you?" Robles said.

"Never mind about the case."

"But you still got it." Robles' gaze found the cover of the binder Nelson had been reading. It was a classified Pentagon report titled "Terror 2000." Robles reached for it, face lit from within. "What're you thinking about, old man?"

Nelson pulled the binder away. "That's not your concern."

"Who's the one done the killing here?" Robles' eyes challenged, and Nelson could feel the anger simmering between them. His mind edged toward the gun in his pocket. Not now. Not yet.

"We don't have time for this," Nelson said.

"Tell me about the binder."

"No."

"It has to do with the case I gave you. With the lightbulbs."

"It's complicated."

"Fuck complicated." Robles pulled his knife from the wall. The blade flashed between them, and Nelson drifted his hand toward the gun.

"You gonna use that thing, you better make it count," Nelson said.

Robles looked at the knife like he'd never seen it before, then shrugged. "I get it, old man."

"Maybe you do."

"Dying's not a problem." Robles spun the knife in his hands and sank it into the wall a second time. "Just don't let me see it coming."

"That's it?"

Robles pointed at the locked door. "And let me do what I want with the girl."

"Actually, that's the other thing I wanted to talk about."

The two men walked over to a window covered in sheer plastic and looked down at what remained of Cabrini-Green's once-notorious nightlife. In a breezeway, a solitary figure huddled against a stiffening wind, waiting for someone to drive up and buy his drugs. Half a block down, a woman stamped her feet against the cold and smoked a cigarette while a second walked small circles under a streetlight. After a while the men moved away from the window and made their plans. Then Nelson left. Robles smoked his own cigarette down and looked up at a starless sky. When he was finished, he got a length of rope, some tape, and his knife. He went over to the locked door and opened it with the key. The girl screamed, but only for a minute. After that Robles had all the time in the world. Or at least until Nelson returned.

CHAPTER 13

Evergreen Park never changes. Row after row, block after block, the brick bungalows march on, each a story and a half high, each featuring a Post-it-size backyard, each identical to the next save for the number on the front that tells the mailman where to leave what. I parked at the corner of Albany and Ninety-fourth and walked a half block until I found the house I was looking for. The shades were pulled tight, and there was no answer when I rang the bell. I took out a card and slipped it under the door.

I was almost back to my car when the curtain I'd been waiting for twitched next door. It's the way things work on the Irish South Side—from the cars people drive to the newspapers they tuck under their arms; the cut of their clothes and the length of their hair; the shape of their faces, and, of course, the color of their skin. All of it is filtered through the curtain that covers over the South Sider's front window. Tells people everything they need to know before they ever open their door and bid the stranger a cautious hello.

I walked toward the house with the nervous curtain and hoped I'd passed muster. The door cracked its seal even as I reached for the buzzer. I could smell mothballs and peppermint. A small pink face peeked out and a pair of bright blue eyes blinked.

"Hi," I said. "I'm looking for your neighbor, Jim Doherty."

The door opened another three inches to reveal a head of white hair.

"You looking for Jimmy?" the old woman said.

I nodded. "He's an old police buddy of mine. Thought I might catch him in."

The woman moistened her lips at the new morsel of information. I was now a cop, which helped a lot in this neighborhood.

"What's your name?" she said.

"Michael Kelly."

The door creaked all the way open. "Peg McNabb. Come on in."

She walked back to a yellow couch covered in plastic. I sat in a matching yellow chair, also covered in plastic. A TV ran WGN's news in the corner with the sound muted. A clock ticked on one wall, and a couple of crucifixes framed a picture of JFK on the opposite wall. Underneath the picture was a small table, with a Bible and some holy water in a glass bottle. Peg had her dinner, a sliver of gray meat, potatoes, and peas, on a metal tray in front of her.

"He's not home," she said and gummed down a mouthful of spuds.

"Any idea when he might be back?"

"Not sure." Peg cut off a small piece of meat and chewed it up in quick bites. Then she raised her head and howled, "Denny."

Her voice summoned forth two creatures from the darkness beyond the hallway. The first was an old man, long and alabaster white, wearing a blue T-shirt and red pajama bottoms. He had a toothpick in his mouth, thick dark glasses perched on his nose, and a can of Old Style hanging loose in one hand. The second figure was an echo of the first, right down to the plastic glasses and beer, except he was thirty years younger.

"This is Denny and Denny Jr.," Peg said. "Junior's just visiting."

I nodded at the pair of them. Life sometimes moved in a closed and curious circle on the South Side.

"He's looking for Jim." Peg's duty done, she turned up the volume on the TV. Tom Skilling was telling us it was still warm for this time of year, but probably going to get colder. Peg grumbled at Tom under her breath. Her husband took a seat on the couch. Her son wandered back to the kitchen and, presumably, dinner.

"You looking for Jimmy?" Denny McNabb wrinkled his already wrinkled forehead.

"He's an old cop buddy of mine," I said.

"Chicago cop?"

"Yeah. I was on the force with Jim just before he retired."

"I was gonna say, you're kind of young to have been working with old Jim."

Denny grinned at his own cleverness and looked over to his wife for a bit of silent applause. Peg ignored him, as the five-day forecast was on. The old man found some solace in his can of beer and returned to our conversation.

"Jimmy comes and goes. We always say he's retired, but you'd never know it. On the go, all the time."

I nodded. "Any idea when he might be back in town?"

"I didn't say he was out of town."

"Is he in town?"

"Saw him this morning, didn't we?" Peg bobbed her head in confirmation, and Denny Sr. continued, "He waved hello. Jumped in his car and was off. Well, speak of the devil."

True to his South Side roots, Denny was keeping an eye on the front window. There, through the curtain, was Jim Doherty, large as life, rolling through the night and up the front walk. Denny pulled the door open before Doherty had made it halfway to the stoop. I stepped out. My pal shook his head and laughed.

"Jesus H. Christ. Michael Kelly." Doherty held out his hand, and I grasped it. The grip was rough and strong.

"You looking for me?" the retired cop said.

"Sort of," I said. "How did you know?"

"I didn't. Just thought I'd stop in and say hello to these two. That your car?" Doherty jerked a thumb toward the street.

I nodded. "These folks saw me at your door. Kind enough to help me track you down."

Denny and Peg hopped around Jim Doherty like he was Irish royalty, if such a thing exists.

"Thanks for hauling him in here," Doherty said.

Denny nodded. "Told him you'd be around, Jimmy." The old woman moved aside to let Doherty into the house.

"No, no, Peg. Michael here is a busy man." Doherty glanced my way. I nodded in agreement.

"I'm just going to take him over for a cup of tea and a chat. I'll come by tomorrow and we can catch up." Jim winked at the couple and nudged me down the walk. I felt their eyes on my back as I moved away. Doherty swung his arms by his sides and laughed as we walked.

"Fuck's sake, Kelly. You get inside that house, you'll be lucky to come out at all. I'm here."

The ex-cop turned down his driveway, toward the back door. On the South Side, front doors were for first-time visitors. Everyday traffic knew better and went around back.

"You want some tea," Doherty said and hung his coat on a hook in the kitchen. I shrugged. Doherty steered me toward a large table.

"Sit down. I got what you want in the other room."

"You know why I'm here?"

Doherty used a match to light the stove and put on a kettle. "Course I know why you're here. Now sit down. You're making me nervous."

CHAPTER 14

"You look good, Michael."

I hadn't seen Jim Doherty in maybe five years, since the day he retired and we drank Guinness together at a pretty good Irish place called Emmit's. I'd meant to call him. Even made notes for myself. But never got to it.

"Thanks, Jim. It's been a while. How you doing?"

Doherty widened his eyes in mock surprise. The smile that followed wiped away my years of neglect.

"No complaints, actually. In fact, retirement suits me pretty well."

Doherty waved a hand around the house. His bungalow was identical to his neighbors', except this one didn't feature a cru-cifix, or even JFK, on the wall. In fact, the whole house felt bare. No pictures, no paintings. Just a few shelves, heavy with books. Otherwise, only what was needed to live.

"I know," he said, "it looks depressing. Some pots and pans and an old cop waiting to die. Right?"

I shook my head. Doherty, however, was never one to cut corners.

"Bullshit. That's exactly what it looks like, because maybe

that's exactly what it is. And you know what? It's not all that bad."

My friend cast pale blue eyes into a future most of us try hard to ignore. His features seemed finer than I remembered; his skin, tissue thin and stretched tight over his skull.

"But you're not here for that sad story, are you, Michael?" Doherty glanced at the thick brown files he'd placed on the table between us.

"You think I'm crazy?" I said.

He shrugged. "What's crazy? In this game, you get hunches. Tell you the truth, I kind of thought the same thing myself."

"Yeah?"

"Yup. First thing jumped in my head when I heard about the shootings in the Loop. Same date. Same place." Doherty leaned in so I could hear the wheeze in his voice. "And I was there, Michael. Don't forget that."

He straightened his spine and stirred some sugar into his tea. "You got any other connections?"

"Actually, I do."

Doherty squeezed his eyes a fraction. He hadn't joined the force until he was in his thirties and never made it past sergeant. Still, the Irishman possessed a subtle thread of intelligence. The kind that made you wonder sometimes if you were playing checkers while he was quietly playing chess.

"I knew there had to be more," Doherty said. "Said that to myself the minute I saw your face pop out of the house next door. I said, 'That fucking Kelly. He's running down those old streets again.' "

Doherty flipped open one of the files and thumbed through a stack of photos as he talked. The fingers were still thick and hard. The hands of a cop. Retirement or no. "So what else do you got, son?"

"I was on the platform at Southport this morning," I said.

"The first shooting?"

I nodded. "Chased the guy for a couple of blocks."

"Didn't catch him, I take it?"

"He caught me up in an alley. Put a gun on me, but didn't pull the trigger."

Doherty put down the old photos and rubbed an index finger along his lower lip. "And you think he was laying for you?"

"I know he was. After the second shooting, he called me."

"The shooter called you?"

"I'm thinking there's two of them, but, yeah, one called. Hit me on my cell phone."

Doherty chuckled. "Fucking balls. What did he say?"

"Bragged about the killings. All that sort of bullshit. But he called me by name and knew a little bit about me. Mentioned Homer."

"Homer? As in *Iliad* and *Odyssey* Homer?"

"One and the same."

The Irishman walked to the sink and considered his reflection in a window. "And you're wondering if this could all tie into the old case?"

"That's why I'm here, Jim."

He poured some more hot water into his mug and sat down again with the files. "I always kept track of this one, Michael."

"I know. You keep in touch with any of them?"

"Some are dead. Some just old. Their sons, daughters . . ." Doherty shrugged off a generation. "They don't always feel it like they would have. You know what I mean?"

I nodded. There was no substitute for being there. "So you think there's no connection?"

"I didn't say that. There could be. Or maybe it's just a coincidence. Maybe these guys are using you as some sort of decoy."

"That's what the feds think."

"FBI?"

"They're running the case. I met with them today."

"What about Chicago PD?"

"They got a man at the table, but the feds are calling the shots."

"Tread lightly, Michael."

"I hear you. What does your gut say on the connection?"

"Honestly?" Doherty tickled his fingers across the files. "I think all of this bothers you more than you want to know. Always has, for some reason."

"And so I see ghosts?"

"Could be. Is the Bureau letting you in?"

"Bits and pieces but, mostly, no."

"So you want to run this down all by yourself?"

"I could use a fresh set of eyes, if that's what you're asking."

"I wasn't. These eyes are past their prime. And I was never even a detective to begin with."

"You were good enough to be one, and you've lived with this case your whole life."

Doherty's chuckle faded to nothing. "You're welcome to whatever I have. If you get a crazy idea you want to run by someone, I'm here."

"But otherwise?"

"Otherwise, I'm old. I know that sounds lame, but, believe me, you'll get there someday and know what I'm talking about. Besides, I have you to do my bidding."

"Fair enough, Jim."

It was an effort, but my friend managed a smile. "Good.

Now let me walk you through this stuff and get you the hell out of here."

Then Jim Doherty opened up a file. It was full of papers and pictures. Full of the future, staring up at me through my past.

I WAS NINE YEARS OLD *and sat in the last seat on the second-to-last car of Chicago's Brown Line, listening to the creak of steel and wood, swaying as the train rattled around a corner, watching the Loop's gray buildings slide past. A man sat across the aisle from me. He had a thin face he kept angled toward his shoes, a long black coat, and his hands jammed into his pockets. Three rows down was a young couple, their heads thrown together, the woman wearing a thick green scarf and glancing up every now and then at the route map on the wall.*

The train jolted to a stop at LaSalle and Van Buren. I snuck a look as the conductor came through a connecting door in the back, pressed a button, and mumbled into the intercom. His voice sounded stretched and tinny over the cheap system. Something about the Evanston Express. His red eyes moved over me without a flicker. Then he craned his head out the window, looked down the platform, and snapped the car doors shut. As the train started to move again, the conductor disappeared into the next car, and the thin man slid into the seat next to me.

"Hey, buddy."

I didn't say anything. Just tightened my fists and felt a patch of dryness at the back of my throat.

"Kid, you hear me?"

I gripped the handle of the hammer I kept in my pocket

and focused my mind on the piece of bone where his jaw hinged. That's where I'd go. Right fucking there.

"Where you getting off?" The thin man shifted closer, fingering the sleeve of my jacket, pressing me farther into the corner. I caught a flash of teeth, eyes rippling down the car to see if anyone was watching. His collar was loose around his throat and a blue-gray stubble ran down his jaw and cheeks. Underneath the scruff, the skin looked rough and scored.

"Fuck off, mister." I tugged my sleeve free and started to pull the hammer out of my pocket. It wasn't the best solution, but at least it was certain. And that felt good.

"Are you all right, young man?" The woman with the green scarf had moved softly. Now she stood in the aisle, close to us, eyes skimming over the thin man who burned with a bright smile.

"I'm fine, ma'am." I slipped the hammer back in my pocket. "Just gonna change seats."

Her face was plain and broad, with blunt angles for chin and cheeks and a short flat nose. Not a beautiful face, but open and honest. Maybe even wise. It lightened when she heard me speak, and I felt a warmth I would have enjoyed if I'd known how scarce a childhood commodity it would turn out to be.

As it was, I moved past the thin man without touching him and took a seat two rows closer to the front. Just across from the woman and her friend, face muffled in the folds of his coat. The conductor had returned to the back of the car, eyes closed, head against the window, bouncing lightly to the tune of train and track. And that was how we sat as our train approached a sharp bend at the corner of Lake and Wabash.

CHAPTER 15

Jim Doherty and I pieced through the past for an hour, maybe more. At a little after ten, I headed back to the North Side, my friend's files in hand. I eased my key into the lock and cracked open the front door to my flat. Didn't make a sound. Didn't matter a bit. She was there, waiting on the other side, wagging her entire body in a spasm of greeting. I dropped to a knee and scooped Maggie up. The springer spaniel was a year old, but still seemed like no weight at all. She licked my face where she could find it and then scrambled out of my arms. I stepped back and watched as a blur of liver, gold, and white sprinted once, twice, three times around the living room, leaped to the couch, and stopped dead still, staring at me, tongue out, panting lightly, body wag still in full flower. I crouched so I was eye level with the pup and feinted like I was going to make a run at her. She offered a head fake to my left and tore off to the right, into the kitchen. I heard the clatter of claws on tile and then a slide and thump into what I suspected was the refrigerator. A second later, Maggie was back in the living room, bearing down on me at full speed. I dropped to a knee and caught her in midleap. She curled into my chest and almost immediately settled. I found a seat on

67

the couch. Five minutes later, the pup was asleep. I sat that way for a half hour. The best half hour of my day. Then I moved lightly. Maggie opened her eyes and stretched. She jumped down to the floor, shook herself once, twice, and wagged her tail, looking up at me, wondering what was for dinner.

DINNER WAS a cheeseburger and a cold can of beer. I steamed some spinach to make myself feel better. Then I gave most of it to the dog. She didn't like it, either. I put a call in to Rachel Swenson's cell phone, but got her voice mail and left a message. My favorite judge still had her own place on the Gold Coast, but spent a good part of the week at my apartment. It felt good to have her here, to see her clothes strewn around the bedroom, my bathroom cluttered with atomizers and smoothers, exfoliants and lotions, peelers and masks. I didn't know what most of it was for, but it didn't matter. Between Rachel and the pup, my apartment was full. And the emptiness I never really knew existed, gone. Or at least put away for a while.

I found the pup's leash and took her for a quick tour of the neighborhood. Then I settled in at my desk and powered up my Mac. The CTA shootings dominated Google's news page. I searched for my name, but didn't get a hit in any of the articles. Good. I shut down the link and sat in the dark, watching the wind batter my front windows. Outside, the night offered an inky canvas on which to replay the day's events: a woman dropping to the hard boards of the Southport L, surprise scratched all over her face; an alley, tunneling through the black and filling up with snow; a tangle of footprints and

the fat hole of a .40-cal pressed to my head. Slipping underneath was the electric silk of the voice on my cell phone, one
that called me by name, one I couldn't place. I closed my eyes
and let the images play. Pretty soon I started to nod off, the
pup close by, readily following my lead.

CHAPTER 16

Five miles south, Nelson rolled to a stop underneath a cement overpass near the corner of Jefferson and Congress. A twist of snow blew across the hood of his Impala and dissolved into cold smoke. Overhead, the Eisenhower hummed with the whine and thump of rubber on asphalt. Nelson looked at the envelope on his dashboard, addressed to his favorite reporter. Then he put on his gloves and cracked open the driver's-side door.

The parking lot wasn't much more than an afterthought, shoved under the highway between the Clinton Blue line stop and the Greyhound bus station. During the day it was filled with the cars of Loop workers who couldn't afford downtown parking. At night, it became a black hole. Tonight was no exception. A brown Ford with a cracked windshield and rims for tires sat in a far corner. Otherwise, Nelson had the place to himself.

He moved out from under the highway and took a slow walk around the block. The bus station had a single cab out front, motor running, driver asleep in the front seat. The rest of the buildings on the street were factories, locked up for the night. Nelson ducked back under the overpass and moved past his car to a far wall abutting the L station. There he found a green door with black stenciled letters that read CTA.

Nelson turned his back to the wind and pulled out the keys he had made. The third one fit, and the door opened. He stepped out of the weather and into a greasy darkness. Nelson found a light switch and flipped it on. A stairwell uncoiled to his left, down and into the belly of Chicago's subway system.

Nelson walked back outside, popped the trunk on the Impala, and considered a local prostitute named Maria Jackson, smiling red at him through the thick plastic. Robles had done a good job wrapping her after he'd finished, and the blood did not seem to have leaked. Nelson took a last look around, lifted the body, and carried it inside. Then he drove his car two blocks and parked on a deserted section of street. From the backseat he pulled a duffel bag. Inside it was a rifle, his scopes, and the hard black case he'd taken from Robles. Nelson hiked back to the access door and opened it again. Maria hadn't gone anywhere. He hefted her body across his shoulders, duffel in his right hand, and began to walk down the first staircase.

NELSON TOOK HIS TIME, resting frequently. Two flights of stairs and a long sloping ramp threaded him back toward the Loop and deep into the lower levels of the subway. A second door opened out to the first run of tracks, an auxiliary spur reserved for trains in need of repair. Nelson walked another hundred paces before allowing the body to slip from his shoulders. Maria Jackson fell among the cinders with a graceless thump. Nelson kept moving.

A quarter mile later, he stopped again. The auxiliary track

split here. Nelson took the right fork and came to a second set of tracks. This was a primary set for the Blue Line's run into the Loop.

Nelson stepped gingerly across the rails and onto the main track. He would hear the train well before it came around the bend, roughly two hundred yards away. Besides, he didn't figure the job to take long. The track Nelson was standing on was the oldest usable section in the entire CTA. It had been scheduled for renovation in 2004. The work had been delayed once, twice, and now, in 2010, still hadn't been done. Which was why Nelson was here. Unlike the other three hundred miles of subway track, this portion had not been updated with sealed fluorescent lighting. Nelson looked up at the bare lightbulbs. Heavy-duty, yes, and partially shielded with steel covers. But lightbulbs all the same.

Nelson found the ladder he knew they kept in a maintenance shed and positioned it under a bulb. Then he took Robles' black case out of his duffel, climbed the ladder, and unscrewed the bulb from its porcelain fixture. He knew this fixture well. He'd bought a half dozen like it from a man who collected CTA odds and ends. Nelson knew it took six turns to secure the bulb in the fixture. Four turns and it would still be all right. Three turns and the vibrations from passing trains would begin to turn the bulb in its grooves and eventually loosen it. Fewer turns . . . or more vibrations . . . and the bulb got looser that much more quickly. An inexact science, with an inevitable result.

Nelson opened the case and took out one of the two bulbs stored inside. Carefully he screwed it in. One and one-half turns. The bulb was now, essentially, a timing device. Depending on how many trains rattled by, the bulb would loosen itself in anywhere from seven days to a couple of weeks. Then it would fall and smash on the steel tracks below. Nelson held out his hand again, felt the oily breeze flowing across his fingertips, and looked up at the huge black vents connecting this section to the rest of the subway system. He climbed down the ladder and checked his watch. Robles was supposed to deliver the package at 2:00 a.m. Plenty of time. One more bulb down the line and Nelson would find a good place to hide, a good place from which to hunt.

CHAPTER 17

I opened my eyes and looked around my living room. The sound was small, but certain. I tapped a key on my sleeping computer. The screen pulsed in the dark: 2:06 a.m. I picked up my gun because it felt like the thing to do, walked to my front door, and considered the thin bar of light peeking out from underneath. Then I opened the door. Sitting in the hallway was a plain brown package, no name on it, wrapped in string. I padded down the hall to a small window looking out over Lakewood. The street was empty. I took the stairs softly, found nothing in the lobby, even less in the basement. I went back upstairs, checking each floor in turn. Whoever my messenger was, he was no longer in the building.

I had left the front door ajar. Maggie was in the hall, sniffing at the package.

"Something to eat, Mags?"

She gave me a hopeful look and went back inside. I followed. The package felt like a book. I cut the string and found it to be exactly that. A copy of the *Iliad*. I opened it up and found the poem's opening lines highlighted and circled:

Sing, goddess, the anger of Peleus's son Achilles and its devastation, which put pains thousandfold upon the Achaeans . . .

I felt around inside the package and found two more items. The first was a cardboard cutout of a train on a black set of tracks, running across a background of yellow. The second was a small map of a subway system, with a key taped to it and an address attached. I took a long look at the map and then jumped on the computer. Twenty minutes later, I was driving through Chicago's sleeping streets, brown package on the front seat beside me.

I HELD A FLASHLIGHT in one hand and my gun in the other. The address attached to the key had taken me to the corner of Clinton and Congress. The key opened a CTA access door tucked under the Ike, near the Clinton L station. A couple sets of stairs and a long ramp brought me to a second door and a run of tracks somewhere in Chicago's subway system. The room itself felt vast. Dull ribbons of steel ran off ahead of me. A string of lights kept the dark canopy above me nailed in place.

I found a wall and moved along its edge until I came to a small alcove formed by two concrete pillars. I stepped just inside and crouched, spreading my map on the ground. Best I could tell, the door I had passed through was marked with a star. Due east was a second spot, marked on the map with a black x and the word BODY in blue Magic Marker.

I put the map away, took out my gun again, and nudged forward. I'd expected the L's thunder, imagined maybe even having to duck a couple of trains, but the place was quiet. As if to underscore the point, a low rumble drifted in and away. I stayed close to the wall, my light playing on the steel to my right. Chicago's trains were powered by an electrified third rail, six hundred volts of direct current. I'd try to keep a healthy distance.

Thirty yards farther, I saw the body. It had been dumped in the middle of a rail bed. I stepped carefully across the tracks and squatted close. The woman was wrapped in plastic, dressed in jeans and a Chicago Bears sweatshirt. Her hands were taped behind her back, and it looked like her throat had been cut. There wasn't much I could do without touching things, so I took a step back, careful to avoid the blood that had pooled underneath. I ran my light up and down the tunnel and wondered why I'd been summoned. Then I stepped off the tracks and found out.

The red dot flicked ahead a few feet, then skipped behind me. I dove for a crevice in the subway wall just as a round clipped the concrete somewhere above my head. I hugged the ground hard and lifted my face an inch or so. The red dot danced in the air, inviting me to come out and play. Then it moved up and over my body. Seconds hung, stretched, and fell. Each breath, an exercise in eternity. The shooter was using some sort of low-light targeting scope and a laser, knew exactly where I was, and could take me out at his leisure. I told myself to stay down, crouch deeper into whatever cover I could find, even as I felt myself lift. Whoever he was, he could kill me whether I stood or hid behind my hands. The last part of that equation, however, I could control. So I stood. Then I took a step. I felt the shake in my boots, and took a second step.

Another round kicked up maybe a foot to my left. I flinched

back into the wall, into cover that was not. Fear churned up and I used it to create resolve. I pushed away from the wall and walked back toward the door from which I'd entered. This time there was a whine and a ribbon of white sparks. A round had caught some steel and ricocheted away.

Unbidden, the face of an eleven-year-old girl jumped up in my mind. She'd been skipping rope outside a high-rise in the Robert Taylor Homes when a stray round off the pavement caught her in the head. I was a rookie cop and the first unit to respond. Her mom beat on my arms, my face, my badge, my chest. The blood of her daughter covered us both. The girl, however, was past caring.

I pushed the image away and kept walking alongside the track, edging down the long curved tunnel. I figured maybe he wasn't going to kill me, unless he just wanted to play a little first. So I kept walking, concentrating on each breath, the rise and spread of my ribs, the feel of the air on my skin, and the grit under my shoes. Then I was at the door, opened and closed behind me. Breath came in a cold rush, flooding my lungs, causing my heart to freeze and thump in my chest. I sat back against a wall and listened. Somewhere above me I heard the echo of a second door opening and closing. The access door at street level. My shooter had just left the building, his point made and received.

LAKE SHORE DRIVE

CHAPTER 18

Robles was up with the sun, drinking coffee and checking his gear. He'd only gotten two hours of sleep, but it would do. Thirty minutes later, he was walking across a soccer field, stiff with morning frost. Robles hefted the bag slung across his shoulders and grunted. The sky was just starting to lighten over the lake, and he could see the cold billow as he breathed. A woman and her dog materialized, maybe twenty yards away, jogging slowly down one side of the field. Robles kept his head down as their paths crossed. The jogger moved off the field and disappeared beneath an overpass. Robles waited five minutes. The jogger didn't return and the field was empty. He moved up a small incline and down the other side, to a sheltered stretch of ground. Spread out before him were eight lanes of highway, flowing north and south. Lake Shore Drive, dark and quiet, maybe forty-five minutes from rush hour.

Robles zipped open his duffel and pulled out a tripod. A couple of cars cruised by, headlights still on, heading toward the Loop. Robles took out a Nikon D300 SLR camera, fitted it to the tripod, and screwed on a zoom lens. Then he zipped up the bag and stashed it behind a stand of trees to his left. Robles looked through the viewfinder and adjusted the focus. A woman and a small child popped into view. Robles glanced up. They were coming straight at him, driving an SUV down a nice, long stretch of road. Robles looked back through the viewfinder and counted off the seconds in his head. One, two, three . . . The woman was smiling and drumming her fingers on the steering wheel. Four, five, six . . . Robles could just make out the top of the kid's head above the dashboard. Seven, eight . . . He looked up again. The SUV blew past in a puff of morning mist. Robles smiled. Perfect. He lensed a few more cars. Got timings for all eight lanes, but focused mostly on the traffic coming toward him. When he was done, Robles snapped a few general photos, wide-angle stuff, just in case anyone happened by and wondered why he was there. A photo documentary project. Then Robles crouched back among the trees and waited. For the traffic to build. And his cell phone to buzz.

CHAPTER 19

I woke up and smelled the coffee. Literally. There was someone in my house, and they were making a pot of joe. Whoever it was, at least they had the good sense to use my stash of El Diablo beans. Now if they'd only bring me a cup.

The second time I woke, the smell was stronger and the intruder closer, as in over my bed, cup in hand, smiling. Simply dream and ye shall receive.

"You're here," I said.

"I let myself in." Rachel Swenson put my coffee on the night table, leaned in, and kissed me. I'd gotten home at a little after four. I looked at the clock on my nightstand. It read 6:50.

"You staying or going?" I said.

"Going. I've got an early meeting."

"I'm thinking they can get along without you."

Rachel's smile was fragrant, even as she shook her head no. I ran my hand down her hip and imagined the slightest bit of maybe. That, of course, was the time Rodriguez picked to call.

"Hello," I said.

"You sound like hell."

"Fuck you. I just woke up."

The detective chuckled. "You ready to go?"

"Go where?"

"Lawson wants to meet us this morning at the Southport L. They finished processing the scene, but she's going up for another look."

"I told Hubert Russell I'd meet him for coffee."

"You bringing him in on this?"

"Could be. Why don't you tag along? Save me the trouble of explaining things twice."

"Explaining what?"

"Filter on Milwaukee. You know where it is?"

"Sure."

"Eight a.m. We can talk then."

I hung up. Rachel sat down beside me and I held her for a good thirty seconds. If I were smart, we never would have moved.

"Sounds like we both have full days," she said, leaning back and studying my face.

I hadn't had time yesterday for anything except a quick phone call, telling her I was involved in the thing at Southport and would explain later. Later, apparently, was now.

"What do you know?" I said, dropping my head back to the pillow.

"Well, I'm guessing you were the eyewitness the police are talking about in the Southport shooting."

"It's a little more complicated than that."

"I'm shocked."

"I bet you are."

"Fill me in."

"I can tell you I'm now attached to the task force working the case."

A frown. "Both shootings?"

I propped myself up on one elbow. "Yeah, they're connected. Hey, you know Katherine Lawson?"

Rachel Swenson was probably the smartest person I knew. Certainly the best looking. She was also a sitting judge for the Northern District of Illinois, which meant she knew the feds. Lots of them.

"Sure. Katherine's a bit of a star with the Bureau. You working this with her?"

"I get the feeling I am. Myself and Rodriguez."

"That should be interesting."

I wanted to pursue how and why Rachel found Agent Lawson so interesting. I also wanted to seriously get Her Honor into bed. Unfortunately, it was getting late for both of us.

"Let's make a date," I said.

"Dinner?"

"Tonight. No matter what."

"You cooking?"

"You feeling brave?"

"Seven o'clock, Kelly."

"Bring your appetite, woman."

I finished my coffee and swung my feet to the floor. Rachel touched me on the shoulder. "How deep are you in this thing?"

I heard the twinge in her voice and thought about the night before—my starring role as the duck in a shooting gallery.

"It's a task force, Rach. Probably just sit around a small office drinking bad coffee."

I hustled into the bathroom. Rachel followed.

"You don't need to lie, Michael."

She was leaning against the edge of the door frame. Some part of my brain registered her legs, which were great. The rest of me was in full avoidance mode.

"What do you want to hear?" I began to run water in the sink.

"Really?"

"Go ahead." I bent down and splashed some water around.

"Law school, Michael? Northwestern, Chicago? You'd love it, you'd be done before you know it, and you'd be a hell of a trial attorney."

It was Rachel Swenson's pet project. Trade my gun for a briefcase. Turn Michael Kelly into Clarence Darrow. I toweled my face dry and escaped back into the bedroom.

"I like what I do, Rach." I threw on some jeans and laced up a pair of New Balance 827s. "Even if I'm not any good at it."

"You're very good at it. And that's not the point."

I reached for my gun on the dresser. She caught my empty hand in hers.

"What is the point?" I said, forcing the question through my teeth.

"It's about growing up."

I pulled my hand away and found the gun. "What I do is pretty grown up." I clipped the nine to my belt.

"That's not what I meant."

I sat down on the bed. She didn't join me this time. "What I do is different."

"What you do is dangerous." Rachel loved to make lists. Now she ticked off my deadly sins on her fingers as she talked. "You work alone. No, you don't work. You hunt. That's what you do. You hunt human beings. Human beings who often hunt human beings themselves. You carry a gun and routinely use it. You have no backup, no safety net. I don't even know if you have health insurance. Worst of all, you like it."

"And?" When overwhelmed by opposing forces, I liked to reach for the reliable conjunction.

"And where does it end? What's the career path here?"

"You mean do I end up getting a bullet in the neck for my trouble?"

"Yes, Michael. That would be nice to know. And it's not just you anymore. You understand that?"

The pup trotted into the room on cue, jumped up into Rachel's lap, and stared at me.

"Nothing I do is going to hurt you." I gestured around the room. "Hurt us."

"You don't know that."

"Yes, I do."

"How?"

"How what?"

"How can you make that promise? How can you say that and not know it's a lie?"

I turned my eyes down again, found my watch. "Listen, Rach, I gotta run. Hubert Russell is waiting and Vince might just start shooting things."

I winced at the choice of words, but Rachel didn't seem to notice. I kissed her on the top of the head, packed up Jim Doherty's files, and left.

As usual, the judge had all the right questions. As usual, I had nothing but jokes for answers.

CHAPTER 20

Filter was in a section of the city called Bucktown. The neighborhood got its name from the goats Polish immigrants used to tie up in their front yards. Today the goats are gone, replaced by angst-ridden hipsters, spiked goths, and dewy-eyed emos. Pick a label and throw a blanket over them: what you have are a collection of just-out-of-college types, living in industrial lofts bought with what was left of their dad's cash, specializing in self-awareness and taking it all very seriously. Think yuppies with tattoos and no sense of humor.

I sat at a table near the window. My waitress stumbled her way across the floor on black platform shoes, wearing ripped jeans stuffed to overflowing and a T-shirt that read WE NEVER SLEEP. She was texting on her cell phone as she set down my cup of coffee.

"Could I get a pierogi with this?"

The woman nodded and began to wander away. Then she looked up from her phone and wrinkled her nose.

"A what?" She spoke in that flat, loud, cringe-inducing tone Americans are beloved for the world over.

"A pierogi. It's a Polish dumpling."

"We don't have them. We have carrot muffins."

I was about to launch into the history of Poles in Chicago, and pierogis in particular, when the waitress's cell phone came alive in her hand, bleating out the theme song from *Sanford and Son*. She beamed at her ring-tone choice as if it were a newborn and then returned to the unappetizing prospect of her job . . . and yours truly.

"Listen, sir, I have things to do. You want something else?"

Hubert Russell drifted into view—baggy jeans, red sneakers, and backpack a perfect fit for the Filter vibe.

"My friend behind you might want something," I said.

The waitress rolled her eyes and flipped open her still-singing phone. "I'll call you back." She hung up without waiting for a response. Then she took Hubert's order for chai tea and moped away.

"What did you do to her?" Hubert settled into a chair across from me and pulled off a chili-red stocking hat. Underneath was a mop of black hair, tied back in a small ponytail.

"Nothing. How you doing?"

"Okay." Hubert began to unpack what I assumed was a nuclear-powered laptop. He kept his body turned away from me and his head slouched low between his shoulders. I knew there was a problem. Then the light coming through the window shifted and I knew why.

"What happened to your face?"

A shiver of anger settled in his jaw. Hubert turned toward me and blinked out of one eye. The other was partially closed and that was the good news. He had a ragged run of stitches holding together the upper half of his eyelid and swelled up into his brow. The left side of his lower lip had caught some thread too, and I bet whatever had happened might have cost him some teeth.

"Was it just fists or something else?" I said.

"No offense, Mr. Kelly, but I don't want to talk about this."

"Not how things work, Hubert. You look out for your friends. And your friends look out for you."

"Maybe I don't need looking out for?"

"Really. You take care of the truck that hit your face?"

Hubert tried to smile, but it looked like it hurt.

"Let me ask you something," I said. "You want to live your life like this?"

"Like what?"

"Scared, ashamed. Pretending whatever it is, it's not a big deal."

"Not right now, Mr. Kelly." The pleading edge in his voice tugged at the fabric of denial that lay bunched between us.

"We're gonna talk," I said. "Later, for sure."

Hubert took a sip of his tea. "Can we do the case now?"

I shook my head and gave him the bare bones. Most of it he had already picked up from the news.

"We have one at least solid lead," I said. "Guy dumped his rifle in an alley after the shooting downtown."

"He never would have done that if it could have been traced, right?"

"You'd be surprised at how careless these guys can get," I said.

"Guys?"

"We think there are two people operating together."

"Can you tell me what you got on the rifle?"

I shrugged. "Nothing yet. No prints. Feds are running a trace."

Hubert lifted his one good eyebrow. "Speaking of the feds, what do you think I can do that the FBI can't?"

"I know the Bureau," I said. "They're running all kinds of

scenarios, working up a profile, comparing details of the crimes against other cases. All the stuff you'd expect."

"Makes sense to me," Hubert said. "Use your database to look for patterns."

"Yeah, but I'm thinking the guys we're looking for might not fit any of the normal patterns. On top of that, the Bureau can't do anything without discussing it for a day and a half. Meanwhile, these guys keep killing people."

Hubert didn't look like he completely bought the logic, but there was enough there for him to be intrigued. "Do they know about me?"

"I'll talk to the powers that be. Maybe get you some sort of consultant's role."

"And if you can't?"

"It's a free country, isn't it?"

Hubert grinned. It might have been my imagination, but it looked like the smile hurt a little less. "Do I get to carry a badge?"

"No, Hubert. What you get to do is think outside the box. Develop an analysis modeled on factors no one else is taking into account."

"And you think that's where these guys live?"

"I think it's worth a shot. You nose around where they've been . . ." I shrugged. "Maybe they left some footprints."

"Sounds like a plan," Hubert said. "Let's get going."

"One more thing. Last time I asked you to help, there was no real danger. Not so here. These guys like to kill, and they're pretty good at it."

Hubert didn't seem impressed. Then I told him the rest of it: the brown package, the *Iliad*, and my trip into the under-world from the night before.

"This guy actually set you up?" Hubert said.

I nodded.

"And shot at you?"

"That was the general idea I got, yes."

"Wow. Are you going to report the body?"

"If they don't find it soon enough, I'll make a call."

"But, for now, you want to keep the package to yourself?"

I smiled. "It was sent to me. I'd like to figure out what it means. So, yes, the package stays between us."

I pulled out the cardboard cutout of the black train over yellow. "This was in there along with the book and the map. I'm thinking it's some sort of logo, but I can't place it."

Hubert picked up the cutout and studied it. "Mind if I hang on to this for a while?"

"So you're still interested?"

"I said I was." Hubert kicked at the pile of documents I had stacked under the table. "Now, when are you going to tell me about all of this?"

I pulled up the files I'd gotten from Jim Doherty. "You're a smart kid."

Hubert had his eyes fixed on the files. "Yeah, yeah. So what surprises do we have here?"

CHAPTER 21

I'd just opened one of the files when Rodriguez walked through Filter's front door. I waved him over.

"I told the detective to meet us here."

Hubert shrugged. "Cool."

Rodriguez slid into the booth beside Hubert. "What's up, kid? Whoa, what happened to the face?"

I thought Hubert might just get up and leave. He smiled instead. "Hi, Detective. How are you?"

Rodriguez looked over to me and back to Hubert. Then he noticed the old files piled up at my elbow.

"What are those?"

Hubert began to type on his laptop. "That is Mr. Kelly's backstory and the reason why we're all here this morning. Would you like to listen now or do you need coffee first?"

Rodriguez got his coffee from the waitress, who wasn't any nicer to him, badge and all. Then he turned his attention to me.

"None of this goes to the task force," I said. "Not until we figure out if there's anything worth looking at."

Rodriguez waved a hand. I tipped open a file and kept talking.

"Thirty years ago, an L train crashed in the Loop. Four cars derailed and wound up in the street. Eleven people were killed."

I threw a spray of old news clips onto the table. Rodriguez picked one up and began to read.

"The anniversary date was yesterday, February fourth," I said. "The crash happened at the corner of Lake and Wabash, site of yesterday's sniper shooting."

Rodriguez looked up. "You been saving all this?"

"I got a pal, retired cop named Jim Doherty. You know him?"

Rodriguez shook his head.

"He was a rookie in '80. Worked the tracks as they pulled bodies out of the cars. Everyone has a case that stays with them. For Jim, this was it. Keeps in touch with the families. Remembers the anniversary. All that stuff. We used to talk about the case when I was on the force."

"Doesn't make sense," Rodriguez said. "Why would anyone start shooting up the L thirty years after the fact? And how does Southport fit? Most important, why put the bull's-eye on you?" The cop took a sip of his coffee. "Too many loose ends."

"There's more," I said and pulled out another news clipping. It was a shot of the Lake Street elevated, moments after the crash. Below lay a tangle of fire trucks, ambulances, and cops surrounding four derailed cars: one lying on its side on Lake Street; one crushing the roof of two parked cars; the other two dangling in that rarefied air, halfway between the tracks and street below.

"I never told Doherty about this." I shrugged. "Not sure why, but I guess I never told anyone."

"Told anyone what?" Rodriguez said.

I tapped my finger lightly on the faded photo. "I was in that one right there."

THE TRAIN TOOK *the curve and I felt it in my stomach. I'd never felt that before, not on this curve, and my nine-year-old brain told me something might be wrong. Wheels chattered high and tight against the steel tracks as the weight of the car fought to swing out over Lake Street. An old lady near the front fell into the aisle with a crack that might have been her wrist. She screamed and someone else screamed to echo her. A man moved to help the lady on the floor. I watched him grasp her upper arm and then they both looked up. I pulled my eyes up, too, just in time to watch us barrel into a second train sitting immobile at the very center of the curve.*

The noise went on forever, a grinding and tearing of metal on metal. This was what a crash sounded like. From the inside out. I slammed into a steel post and rolled across the floor. I blinked away the blood and felt the rip in my forehead. It hurt to stand up, but I did and climbed back toward my seat. Most everyone else was still on the floor. I was sure they were hurt, but there was precious little room for thought as our train continued its climb up the back of the first. Then the noise stopped. Whispers of pain began to bleed through the shock. I looked back toward the thin man. He was out cold, a small gash near his temple and a smear of blood against the window. I grinned to myself. Even at nine, I knew a silver lining when I saw one. I stepped back into the aisle just as another surge of power ran through the train and up into the soles of my sneakers. Once, twice, five times in all, our train seemed to buck and actually accelerate into the train it had already mangled. Each time the accordion effect caused the car we were in to bend and flex. The fifth time was the charm. Our car popped off the tracks, pitched to the left, and fell over the side, toward the street twenty-five feet below.

"HUH." Rodriguez looked at me and waited.

"I was just a kid," I said. "There were a lot of people inside. A few of them died. Most of us got out okay."

"You know anyone who was in the car with you?" Rodriguez said. "Anyone who might hold a grudge?"

I held up a finger. "I knew one person, but he's dead."

"You sure?" the detective said.

I nodded and half smiled. "It was my old man. He was a conductor on the car that night."

I WOKE UP *in darkness, staring down at a strip of white crosswalk painted across Lake Street and crosshatched by a tangle of girders. I tried to stand up and realized that wasn't going to be easy. My feet were above my head, which was jammed into a corner near the rear door of the train. I pushed myself slowly away from the gash that had opened up in the floor and began to crawl up the aisle, toward the back of the car. Two seats away, the thin man was slumped forward now, his body silhouetted by a splash of light sifting down from the tracks. I crawled a little closer. His forehead was caved in, long nose split to the bone. There was a soup of blood and tissue pooled on the seat and his mouth creaked open at the jaw. I looked to the back of the car. There was no one there, just a connecting door standing open and an empty seat where my father had been sitting. I moved toward the door, looking for my own way out. Maybe I moved too fast because the car began to groan in the wind. I froze and the train settled again. I could hear sirens in the distance and then a voice, close by and behind me.*

"Help."

I SHRUGGED and took a sip of coffee. "They lifted me out of the car and put me in an ambulance. Never talked to my old man about any of it—that sounds strange, but you had to know my old man. Never saw anyone else from the train, none of the passengers, ever again."

Rodriguez scratched his chin and picked through the old files. "And you're thinking this is too much coincidence?"

"Once the killer drew me into the case, yeah, that's exactly what I thought."

"But you have no actual connections to what happened yesterday? No one that's alive, anyway?"

I glanced toward Hubert, who was watching closely. "That's where the computer kid comes in. He's going to develop a program that assumes I'm the target and analyzes the data accordingly."

The detective looked up. "What in hell does that mean?"

"It means," Hubert said, "that I take all the information in these files, plus all the current case information you can get me, and see if any of it ties into Mr. Kelly. Compare names, dates, cases he worked. Things like that."

Rodriguez sighed. "Seems pretty thin."

"It's a hunch," I said. "Nothing more."

Rodriguez finished his coffee just as the check arrived. "How long will you take to get up and running?"

"I already am." Hubert smiled. "I hacked into the task force data bank last night and sucked up most of your initial data. Police reports, all that stuff."

"Motherfucker."

"Thanks, Detective. You guys leave me alone and I might have some ideas for you this afternoon."

"Let's go," I said. "Take care of those files, Hubert."

The kid nodded and was already tapping away on his laptop as we left.

CHAPTER 22

Rodriguez put his car in gear and slipped into the morning rush. "What's up with the old files?"

"You don't buy it?"

"I think there's more than just a hunch behind whatever it is you're thinking."

I shrugged. "Don't give me too much credit. Like I said, the feds got all the conventional angles covered."

"And you're just rolling the dice?"

"From my talk with the mayor, sounds like that's what he wants."

Rodriguez pulled up to a red light. "What the mayor wants, Kelly, is no more bodies and a bullet in the head of whoever the fuck is behind this."

The light turned green and Rodriguez pushed through the intersection. "So your old man was on the train with you?"

"That's right."

"You want to talk about it?"

"Not really."

Rodriguez grunted and took a left on Ashland. We drove in silence for a few blocks.

"Where we headed?" I said.

"I told you. Lawson wants us to meet her at the Southport L."

"Are they opening it up today?"

"Wilson insisted. Business as usual."

I turned on the radio. The first words I heard were "CTA sniper." I flipped to another channel and found a woman talking about the CTA "war zone." I flipped again. CNN was promoting its special, "A City under Siege." Wolf Blitzer would broadcast live from the scene of the sniper shooting downtown. I turned off the radio. "Business as usual, huh?"

"You know the rules. If the mayor says the sky is purple and the earth is flat, hell, let's make the best of it. By the way, what happened to the kid's face?"

"Got beat up," I said.

Rodriguez glanced over. "You want me to check it out?"

"What do you think?"

"I can touch base with Hate Crimes."

"I'm guessing their plate's full."

"You got that right. I'll take a run through their open files. See if anything looks familiar." Rodriguez took a right onto Belmont and then a left onto Southport. The L tracks loomed overhead. "Here we are."

The detective slotted his Crown Vic at an angle to the curb, ass end taking up almost half the street. I climbed out of the car and noticed a guy in a Beemer behind us. He looked like he was going to roll down the window and start something. Then Rodriguez popped his blue flashers and slipped out the driver's side. The guy swallowed the half dozen or so "fuck you"s he had lined up and maneuvered his car around us. Rodriguez took no notice.

"Come on," he said. "Let's go."

The detective walked toward the L station. I followed. Life could be good in Chicago, especially when you carried a badge and a gun.

CHAPTER 23

The Southport L station was nothing more than a box of wood with a couple of turnstiles, machines where you could buy a train pass, and a small booth for the CTA lifer, who was typically skilled at yawning and looking bored. Today was no exception.

"Excuse me, ma'am?" Rodriguez flipped open his badge. The woman inside pulled her eyes up off her morning *Sun-Times*.

"Seen plenty of those today, honey." She smiled and winked at me. Maybe because I didn't flash any tin. Then she popped open a gate beside the turnstile. Rodriguez shouldered his way through.

"I'll be right up," I said. The detective grunted and started to climb the stairs. I turned back to the woman, who used long purple fingernails to turn the pages of her paper. She settled on something that looked suspiciously like Michael Sneed's column.

"Not too busy today?" I said. It was half past nine, still rush hour, and I hadn't seen a commuter yet.

The woman snorted, but didn't bother to look up. "Been

here three hours, sweetie. Usually have maybe a thousand come through by this time of morning. Another five hundred by noon. Today . . ."

The woman looked over at a computer screen and hit a few buttons.

"A hundred thirty-five so far. That doesn't include cops." She nodded in the direction of the departed Rodriguez. "Hell, we got more cops up there than commuters. That's for damn sure."

"You here yesterday?" I said.

"Already told your pals. Didn't see much. Just a single pop and a lot of screaming."

"Pretty big deal, huh?"

The woman shrugged. "I live on the South Side, honey. We get people shot up all day, every day." She moved her eyes to the right. For the first time I noticed a small TV. It had the sound turned down and was tuned to Fox's morning news. The extended edition.

"My neighbor has a little girl," the woman said. "Hit by a bullet last summer while she was sitting on her living room floor, putting together a goddamn jigsaw puzzle. Girl's ten years old and gonna spend the rest of her days strapped to a bed. You hear about that on the TV?"

I shook my head. The woman was awake now. Maybe more than I needed, but there it was.

"That's 'cuz it wasn't on the TV. Not so you'd notice, any-way. Listen, I feel bad for that poor woman yesterday. And the girl downtown. I'll pray for them and theirs. But, goddamn, they got an army walking those tracks."

She dropped her eyes to the little screen again. I did the same. A reporter with plastic hair and a freshly painted grin stood at the corner of Eighteenth and Halsted, in the heart of Pilsen. Behind him, kids flashed gang signs and mugged for the camera.

"That's all they talking about this morning. Hispanics gonna demand some answers."

"Hispanics?" I said.

"Sure. The lady up on the platform yesterday was Hispanic. So was the girl downtown. Hispanics say it's a conspiracy. City doesn't give a damn."

The woman in the CTA booth opened her mouth and laughed. Not a pretty, musical laugh, but harsh. A twisted and cramped sort of thing. Filled with anger. Filled with payback.

"City doesn't give a damn about Hispanics. Shit, Hispanics don't know nothin' 'bout being nothin'. Come down to my neighborhood. Don't get no army of cops down there when the black girl gets shot."

The woman was right, at least from where she sat. But there wasn't anything I could do about it, and we both knew it. So she just shook her head.

"The hell am I telling you for? You a cop. You know how it is."

"It's okay," I said.

"Yeah, it's okay for you. Heading up?"

I nodded. She popped the gate a second time and I walked through it. The woman went back to her paper, clicking her nails and humming softly to herself.

Up on top, the platform was deserted—that is, if you didn't count the twelve cops stationed on both sides of the tracks. A uniform stopped me as I got to the top of the stairs.

"I'm going to have to give you a quick pat down, sir."

"No kidding."

"Yes, sir."

"You going to do this with every person taking the L today?"

I saw a touch of anger in the eyes, a flare of the nostrils. A lot of cops don't like it when people ask them questions, especially when they have someone running around shooting people for no apparent reason.

"Yes, sir," the cop said. "Until we get some metal detectors, it's going to be a pat down for every person who wants to ride the train."

I wondered who came up with that brilliant idea, but decided to keep the rest of my thoughts to myself. "I'm here with Detective Rodriguez," I said. "Got a nine millimeter on my hip. The license to carry it is in my back pocket."

The cop took a half step back at the mention of a gun and jerked his hand toward his shoulder mike. I pointed to Rodriguez who had his back to me, about twenty yards down the platform.

"That's Detective Rodriguez right there. Why don't you call him over?"

"Yes, sir, please keep your hands where I can see them." The uniform hadn't pulled his gun yet and shot me, but I figured it to be just a matter of time. Fortunately, Rodriguez picked that moment to turn around.

"He's with me, Officer." Rodriguez motioned me in. The cop studied the detective. Then he stepped aside and I walked across the platform.

"Nice atmosphere up here today," I said.

"What did you expect?"

"I don't know, but this isn't going to work."

"You haven't seen the worst." Rodriguez walked me over to the railing. From Southport the elevated tracks snaked due east, bending down alleys and across people's backyards, before turning south toward the Loop.

"Can you see them?"

Rodriguez pointed to a row of rooftops. I saw them, small mounds, at least one hunkered down at the corner of several buildings along the run of tracks.

"So they really put them in?" I said.

"Yup. Federal snipers, covering selected stations and then scattered along the entire route. They're not fully deployed yet. But, of course, they started here."

"Press is going to love this." I glanced up and down the street. "By the way, where is the Fourth Estate?"

Rodriguez grinned. "Wilson did get his way there. Pushed the fuckers back two blocks and completely off Southport. A security perimeter. No pictures of any of this. No bullshit live shots, either."

I shook my head. "They'll get their pictures and they'll take the city apart for trying to keep them out of it."

Rodriguez turned away from the street. "Right now, no one really cares. The mayor just wants to get through today with no more bodies."

"And you think this is going to work?"

The detective shrugged. "Will it prevent him from hitting us again? Maybe not. But if he hits here, he's a dead man. That much, I can guarantee."

"That's nice to hear, Detective." We both turned to find Katherine Lawson walking toward us, badge around her neck, face pale and pinched. "Kelly, you want to walk with me for a minute?"

Lawson kept moving toward an empty end of the L platform. I fell in step.

"You want to put a bullet in this guy?"

I glanced at Lawson, who kept her eyes straight ahead as she spoke.

"Good morning to you, too, Agent Lawson."

"Answer the question, Kelly."

"I'm guessing a lot of people would like that," I said.

Lawson stopped walking and jammed her hands into her pockets.

"I know it's your mayor's preferred solution," she said. "And I don't think my boss would mind it very much, either. Problem is . . ."

"Problem is, I'm not a hired gun. Even if I was, you have no idea who this guy is, where he is, or what he's going to try next. And, by the way, for my money we're talking two people here."

"Maybe. Rodriguez already knows this, but I wanted you to hear it from me."

"What's that?"

"Most of the team wants you cut out of this investigation altogether."

"And then there's the people who want to put a bull's-eye on my back and use me as bait."

"There is that faction, but the prevailing sentiment seems to be that you're a distraction. Someone this guy picked out to screw up our focus."

"And?"

"And therefore you're going to be discarded."

"At least you didn't snicker when you said it."

"Don't take it personally. Well, maybe you should take it personally. For what it's worth, I disagree with their assessment."

"How so?"

"Sometimes the Bureau skews facts to fit their theory of a case."

"And you think that's what they're doing here?"

"Could be. This guy went out of his way to put you in the game. My gut tells me it's not something we should ignore."

"So how can I help?"

"The phone call yesterday. You said he mentioned something about Homer."

"You mean glory and suffering? Zero-sum game?"

"Yeah, what was that all about?"

"You really want to know?"

"I asked."

"He was talking about the *Iliad* and the ancient concept of honor. According to the Greeks, you only earned honor through action, by defeating your opponent. And your measure of honor was in equal measure to the amount of pain you inflicted."

"Zero-sum game?" Lawson said.

"Exactly."

"So this guy is going to extract as much pain as he can."

"If we were in Greece in the eighth century B.C., yes, that's exactly what he'd do."

"Great. And I assume you have no idea how any of that connects up to what we've got going on here?"

"If it was that easy, I'd have spoken up yesterday."

"Not sure I believe that." Lawson leaned a hip against the railing and looked out over Chicago's rooftops. A federal agent looked back at us through the scope of his weapon.

"People are going to go crazy when they see this," she said.

"Yes, they are."

"I dug a little dirt on you, talked to people who have actually worked with you in the field."

"And?"

"Some say you have good instincts. The rest say you're just lucky. And those are your friends."

"What do you say?"

"I say we need a little luck." Lawson turned her back to the street and folded her arms across her chest. She kept her eyes fixed on the wooden planks of the L platform as she spoke. "It has to be low-key. You work the case as an unofficial consultant. Your contacts are Rodriguez and myself. Above all, you stay away from the main investigation."

"I'm getting that warm, tingling feeling inside."

"You want to do this or not?"

I wanted to tell her about the mayor, about how he had already locked me up as the city's "official" unofficial consultant. But then I figured what the hell, double-dipping was practically a birthright in Chicago.

"You want to pay my daily rate?" I said. "Or a flat fee?"

"Work it out with Rodriguez. If you turn up any leads . . ." Lawson stopped and looked over again. "I mean anything of significance, you report it to me. Immediately. And then we decide what to do together. Are we clear?"

"One more question. Why take the chance?"

"With you?"

I nodded. "My experience with agents from the Bureau is they like to play it by the book. Even when they don't agree with their boss."

"How many female agents have you worked with?"

"You're the first."

"Exactly. The Bureau is only slightly less misogynistic than the Catholic church. Women have to work twice as hard and be three times as smart just to stay afloat."

"And they need to take chances?"

"After a while, you figure, 'Why not?' Especially on the big ones. Now, what are you going to need?"

I held up a finger. "One thing." I wrote down Hubert Russell's name and number. "I need to hire this guy. He's a little unorthodox and not really an investigator, but he understands computers and he understands stealth."

Lawson looked at the name. "Should I meet him?"

"I don't see why."

"What does he do?"

"What do we have so far? A woman shot at close range with a forty-cal, a sniper shooting, and a knife attack. No real pattern, except they all involve the city and, one way or another, the CTA. What else?"

"The bad guy reaches out to you on the phone."

"That's right. So we know he's got an ego. Big surprise. But where's the focus? What's the overall pattern?"

"Maybe there isn't any," Lawson said.

"Maybe not. My guy will create a profile."

"I got a team at Quantico doing that right now."

"Not like Hubert will. Look, it might not work, but I think it's worth a shot."

"When can you get him up and going?"

"He already is."

"Thanks for talking to me first, asshole. Keep me informed."

My new favorite federal agent turned away just as my cell phone buzzed. I reached for it and a half dozen police radios exploded with sound.

CHAPTER 24

I t was 9:45 when Nelson sent his text message. Robles checked it and turned the phone off. The morning rush along Lake Shore Drive was still in full throat, a solid line of cars creeping south at twenty miles an hour. Robles had moved forward a bit so he was under the overhang of a tree and scanned the line of cars with the zoom lens of his Nikon. Then he pulled out a small set of binoculars and gave the road a second look. Robles didn't know exactly what he was searching for: a face, a gesture, a moment, something that would tell him who lived and who died.

At 9:51 he stowed the camera back in his duffel and pulled out a rifle with a scope. He was used to the weapon now and it felt good in his hands. Using the trees as cover, Robles ran over the rifle quickly. He had checked it before he left, but wanted to make sure. Then he loaded it and leaned it against a tree. From his bag, the shooter pulled out a folding bipod and set it up with a clear view of the Drive. He threw a small bean bag behind the bipod, dropped to the ground, and lay there for a minute or more, using his binoculars to review the sight lines a final time.

At 9:55 Robles put his binoculars away and crawled back to

where he'd left the rifle. He slung it over his shoulder and moved forward again to the shooting stand. Gently, he lifted the weapon onto the bipod and seated the rifle butt in the bean bag. The morning sun was glancing off the lake, partially blinding the drivers headed south and providing even more cover. Still, Nelson wanted no more than a minute's worth of shooting time. Robles let out a slow, even breath and eased his eye to the scope.

The first face he saw was that of Jessica Morgan, twenty-three years old and driving a Ford Focus. Jessica was a single mom, working as a paralegal at a Loop law firm and taking classes at night to earn her college degree. Jessica would never know about the law degree she'd have earned from the University of Chicago, her subsequent clerkship with a federal judge, and, eventually, her own seat on the Illinois Supreme Court. Instead, Jessica smiled in Robles' scope and pulled an invisible strand of hair back from her face. Then she got an education in execution. The round shattered her windshield, hit her steering wheel, and struck Jessica just under the chin, killing her instantly. Robles, however, never saw the fruits of his handiwork. The clock was running, and his rifle was searching.

Peter Rubenstein was two cars away, driving an almost new Cadillac Seville. Peter was sixty-three years old and a widower. His wife, Marcy, had died a year and a half earlier when she fell down a flight of stairs in their home. Rubenstein wept at her funeral and sold their house within three months of putting "his Marcy" in the ground. Now he lived in a high-rise condo along the lake, courtesy of his dead wife's insurance cash. Peter was whistling and enjoying a view of the morning sun shimmering off the water. He'd never know his insurance settlement had been flagged by state investigators.

Never know about the order to exhume Marcy's body and the subsequent report that would have established her death as a homicide, the result of several blows to the head "inconsistent with a fall down the stairs." He'd never get to hear the charge of murder laid against his name or feel the cuffs as they slipped across his wrists. He'd never get to know any of that, but he would get to see "his Marcy" sooner than he expected. Robles' second round hit Rubenstein in mid-whistle, just below the left eye, tearing off most of his head and making life miserable for the undertaker when Rubenstein's family insisted on an open casket.

Robles' third shot missed everything. His fourth punched through the chest and burst the heart of forty-seven-year-old Mitchell Case, a second-rate accountant who would never find out about the first-rate affair his wife was having, not to mention the malignant tumor percolating inside his skull. Case's Corolla was traveling at twenty-eight miles an hour when he was struck. The car hit the divider, jumped it, and plowed into a van headed north. That driver, eighteen-year-old Malcolm Anderson, would never meet his daughter, Janine, because she'd never be born. The only passenger in the van, thirteen-year-old Randall Blake, would have his left leg crushed in the wreckage, undergo four hours of emergency surgery at Northwestern Memorial, and survive. Randall would consider himself one of the lucky ones from that day on the Drive. He'd never know about his four years as an All-American guard at the University of Michigan or the Hall of Fame career he would have enjoyed with his hometown Bulls. Never know about the $113 million he'd have earned, the wife he'd have married and grown old with, or the five girls he'd have watched raise families of their own. Instead, Randall would walk for the rest of his life with a limp and a cane.

He'd die alone, at the age of forty-six, from complications due to hepatitis C, the disease of a junkie, which is exactly what Randall would become.

Three cars behind Mitchell Case's car, Robles' final round creased the roof of a black 2009 Audi and caromed away harmlessly. Inside, the driver took no notice of the metallic ping, not with the horror show unfolding in slow motion around her. Rachel Swenson locked her brakes and heard the crunch as she hit the car in front of her. A half beat later, she felt another car plow into her from behind. At the same time her air bag deployed, knocking her silly and preventing her from being impaled on the steering wheel. Rachel put her hand to her face and slipped the rearview mirror over. There was a cut on her forehead, and she felt a little dizzy, but she was alive and still conscious. A car had jackknifed over the divider and a young black boy was halfway out of a van and moaning. She leaned her shoulder against the driver's-side door and popped it open. Then Rachel was up and out of the car. There was a smell of raw gasoline in the air. A few feet away, a man was screaming that he had called the police. Rachel could already hear the sirens. She walked down the line of wrecked cars. In one she could see a man with most of his head missing and a young woman crouched nearby, vomiting. Rachel hadn't spent time at a lot of crime scenes, but she'd seen enough to know the injury she was looking at was not the result of any car accident. The black boy near the van moaned again. Rachel climbed the divider and picked her way around the wreckage. She'd do what she could. As she walked, she felt her cell phone in her pocket. She pulled it out, dialed, and waited for the other end to pick up. That was when she saw the lone figure, across three lanes of highway, packing up a duffel bag and disappearing into a stand of trees.

CHAPTER 25

Rodriguez hit the intersection of Belmont and Racine at fifty miles an hour and climbing. He had his lights and siren on and was typing into a computer built into a console between us. I had just hung up with Rachel and was scribbling down everything she'd told me. Rodriguez finished with his notes and looked over.

"What do you got?"

"She said he was dressed in a dark-colored jacket and maybe jogging pants. Holed up on a little rise of grass, just west of the Drive."

Rodriguez was at sixty now, moving east on Belmont.

"And she thinks he's the guy?"

"She says he was packing a black duffel and running."

"Hold on."

Rodriguez typed a few more lines into his computer. Then he came back to me.

"You all right with this?" he said.

Rachel told me she was okay. She sounded okay. And she let me talk to one of the people on the road with her who assured me she was more than okay. So I let her tell me about the man on the hill. Let her talk me into going after him.

"I'm fine. What are we doing?"

Rodriguez swung a hard right onto Inner Lake Shore Drive. Traffic was at a standstill. Rodriguez cut back west and picked his way south down Sheridan.

"We're setting up a perimeter from Halsted Street east, along the lake from Addison to North Avenue. We're getting some choppers up, and I got the description out there. If he didn't jump in a car, we got a chance."

"How many did he hit?"

Rodriguez shrugged. "Don't know. But it doesn't sound good."

The detective smoked his tires taking a left off Sheridan and gunned it the wrong way down Diversey, to a dead end and a parking lot. It was less than five minutes since the last shot was fired. The lot had three cars in it. All of them empty. Rodriguez and I pulled our guns and moved to the soccer fields that lay just beyond.

"The area she described is just over the hill," Rodriguez said. "I'm gonna go straight up. You circle around to the south. If he's still on foot, there's a chance he headed that way."

Rodriguez was right. If our shooter had headed north or west, he'd have to navigate a half mile's worth of open ground. To the south was the parking lot. Beyond it, cover in the form of winding paths, trees, and a series of underpasses.

"Put me on your net so some cop doesn't shoot me," I said.

Rodriguez nodded. "You're on it. Just don't change clothes on me. Here, take a radio."

The detective threw me a handheld and headed toward the hill. I checked the volume on the two-way to make sure it was squelched and started jogging south along a running path that skirted Diversey Harbor and Lincoln Park Lagoon. Two minutes and a hundred yards later, a dog stood at the top of a small rise, wagging his tail for no apparent reason. I knew a little about dogs. Very little. My pup, however, rarely wagged without a reason, usually because she saw something or someone. I pushed up the incline.

"What do we got here, boy?" I scratched the dog behind the ears. He wagged his tail even harder. Ahead, the jogging path dipped to the left and ran underneath a bridge that spanned Fullerton Avenue. I crept toward the black hole under the bridge. The dog stayed where he was. Smart dog.

CHAPTER 26

Robles wore navy-blue running pants, a blue hooded sweatshirt, running gloves, and a hat. He kept a snub-nosed revolver tucked in one pocket of his sweatshirt and a set of keys in the other. Fullerton Avenue above him was quiet. A chopper beat somewhere in the distance. Robles was twenty yards beyond the bridge when he heard someone call out to the dog. Time was running thin. Nelson had stressed he'd have about ten minutes from his last shot to get to where he needed to be. That was seven minutes ago. Robles could have run for it, but he didn't. Instead he veered off the path, into the scrub alongside the lagoon, and waited. He heard the crunch of gravel, the slosh of water, and the rumble of a garbage can as its cover was removed. A head peeked out from underneath the bridge. Then, a hand and a gun. Robles fired twice. A body fell back into the darkness. Robles looked around. There was a lot of swirl, but it was all still a mile or so north, focused on the tragedy and neglecting the periphery. Just as Nelson had predicted. Robles stood up, brushed the dirt off his pants, and began to jog again. Fifty yards later, he found the building he was looking for, fitted a key into a lock, and disappeared inside.

. . .

THE FIRST ROUND scored the pavement a foot or so to my left. The second knocked me to the ground. I knew I was hit and saw my gun lying in a puddle of water a few feet from my head. I struggled to my feet and wedged myself between a steel girder and a trash can. My right arm wouldn't cooperate, so I reached for the gun with my left. Then I waited for the pain to settle. The air under the bridge was cold and damp. Water dripped down the walls and pooled in the broken cement at my feet. I slipped my hand under my vest. It came away red, but the wound didn't seem too bad. I gave it another ten seconds and crept out again. The running path was empty. Whoever had shot me was gone.

I moved down to the water's edge, slumped into the weeds, and looked out over the lagoon. A couple of ducks looked back. Then they flapped their wings and lifted into the air. Far above them another bird hovered. This one was a police chopper, scouring the shoreline. I waved, but it moved off. The water below was quiet, chunks of ice floating here and there. Around a soft bend in the shoreline, a single boat suddenly appeared, a kayak paddling out from the Lincoln Park Boat House, heading toward the lake. The kayaker wore a hat, gloves, and a dark sweatshirt. It seemed like an odd outfit, but then again, I had never kayaked through a Chicago winter. Didn't know anyone who had.

I inched back a little deeper in the scrub and watched some more. The kayaker was struggling with his stroke, unable to coordinate the lift and fall of the double-bladed paddle. After twenty yards or so, he smoothed out and began to move a little better. I stretched out on my stomach and lay flat on the ground. The man might have caught my movement, because he stopped paddling and leaned forward. For a moment, I saw the short shape of a gun, outlined against the hard winter gray. Then it disappeared back in the bottom of the boat.

I held my nine in front of me with two hands. The blood flowed a little more freely down my side, but the pain had subsided, and my head was clearing. The kayak was moving again, from right to left, maybe fifty yards away. I knew I was at maximum range for my gun and squeezed down over the sight. The boat drifted closer and the shot got easier. I moved the gun from temple to jaw and then down over the mass of the kayaker's body. The mayor's face slipped across the edge of my vision. As did a federal agent, with a badge and a knowing smile. I tightened up another notch on the trigger. Then I exhaled and pushed back into the weeds.

My words tasted like dust, but I radioed in anyway and told Rodriguez about the boat. I could hear the rotor chop above me fade for a moment, then grow louder. They had drifted a bit north, but would arrive in plenty of time to cut off whoever our kayaker was. He continued his slow crawl across the lagoon. I pulled the gun up again and tracked him. Just for fun this time. The kayaker ducked and paddled, still a rough but steady stroke. His face turned once, as if he sensed something, and his profile flashed in a column of light. I lowered my gun. Then I heard a crack, and the kayaker's chest exploded in a cloud of tissue and red.

ROBLES HEARD A POP and felt a tug at his throat. Then he was at the bottom of the kayak, staring up at the sky and choking on his own blood. Robles thought about the girl from last night. He'd enjoyed killing her. This morning on the Drive, even more. He thought about all the others, women struggling against the darkness, children submitting, small graves in the woods. Those were his private treasures. His secrets. Today had been his glory.

Robles' mind emptied, and filled again with a summer day. He was a kid gone fishing. The sun gentled and the boat rocked as the man moved in the bow and then settled, cigarette in one hand, line in the other. Robles remembered the trout he'd caught that day, silver and pink against the roughed-out bottom of the boat. The man gripped the fish, belly down, and hit it twice with the rounded butt of a knife. Then he threw the trout into a rusty hold filled with water. Robles remembered looking into the well, seeing the black eyes peering out from under. Then the lid closed, and the eyes were gone. The man returned to his perch and fell asleep. The boy remained where he was, breathing softly and watching the water move around him.

Such were Robles' thoughts as he looked up at the sky, lungs swollen with blood, police chopper drifting, and then nothing.

CHAPTER 27

I 'm fine," I said, for the fourth time in the last minute and a half. The inside of my mouth tasted like dry wool. I reached for a paper cup and felt the pull of an IV in my arm. The water slipped down my throat, but seemed to have no discernible effect.

"You realize how close you came to dying?"

Rachel was standing beside the ambulance, head bandaged, shoulders hunched, arms crossed. She had been in the middle of Lake Shore Drive, talking to Rodriguez, when I called over on the radio. Then came a report that I'd been hit. She hitched a ride in a squad car and bitched at the cops the whole way. At least, that's what they told me later.

"The bullet caught my vest," I said, showing her the four stitches in my side. "Nothing more than a scratch."

"It's a little more than that, Mr. Kelly." That was the EMT, not making things any easier, so I ignored her.

"How's your head?" I said.

Rachel touched the white bandage at her temple. "My head's fine."

She'd been in the wrong place on the Drive at the wrong

time. Unlucky in some ways, incredibly fortunate in others. Either way, it wasn't my fault, even if I felt like it was.

"Someone taking you down for X-rays?" I said.

She nodded. "Rodriguez said he'd drive me over."

"You okay?"

A smile limped across her face and back into her pocket. "Just tired, Michael."

I took her hand. "I'll call you later."

"Maybe make it tomorrow."

"You sure?"

"You're going to have your hands full here and I just need some sleep."

I kissed her, then watched her walk away. Rodriguez was waiting by his car. He caught my eye and held it. Then he touched Rachel's shoulder. She got in the passenger's side and leaned back against the headrest. Rodriguez climbed in the other side, and they drove off.

I unplugged myself from the IV and stood up. A couple of police choppers still hovered over the lagoon, an effort to keep the flying media away. A police boat had tied up to the kayak. They were offloading the body in a bag. I began to walk toward the shoreline.

"Mr. Kelly, I can't just let you go." The EMT was following me. "You could go into shock and there's a risk of infection."

"Is he giving you a hard time?"

Katherine Lawson trudged up the slope from the lake. Three more agents trailed behind her. Lawson pulled off a set of latex gloves and threw them into a bag that had the word HAZARD stenciled on it.

"What did you find?" I said.

Lawson held up a finger and huddled with the EMT for a

moment. Lawson came back alone. "Thank me, Kelly. I just got you a hall pass."

"Yeah?"

"Yeah." She held out a bottle of pills. "Take four immediately and two a day after that until they're gone. Prevents infection."

"Four right now?"

"That's what she said. How's the side?"

"Your protective vests suck."

Lawson looked over at the garment, folded and lying inside the ambulance.

"That's Chicago PD issue."

"And if I'd been wearing yours?"

"I'd probably be helping Rachel Swenson pick out a black dress. By the way, how is she?"

"She just left. Got banged up a little by the air bag, but otherwise, fine."

"I like her."

"So do I," I said. "Let me ask you a question. Any reason to think she was the target here?"

"You mean was he targeting Rachel to get at you?"

"Something like that."

Lawson shook her head. "Unlikely. If he was, why waste bullets on anyone else? And she was the only one he missed. By the way, here's your gun."

The agent pulled my nine-millimeter from a bag by her feet.

"Thanks." I tucked it into my belt. "So you're thinking Rachel was another coincidence?"

Lawson nodded. Usually I hated to agree with the feds. This time, not so much. We walked a little more until we reached a line of police tape. A not-so-small crowd had gathered beyond.

"I'm guessing you'd like to get out of here?" Lawson said.

"You here to make that happen?"

"Let's go somewhere and talk."

CHAPTER 28

We drove five blocks to a bar called Four Farthings. Twenty years ago, it was a big singles joint in Lincoln Park. Then the crowd got old, which was okay except they forgot to leave. Now the place was mostly filled up with dusty conversations about the good old days from a dried-up clientele who tended to fall asleep after three drinks.

At five in the afternoon there were six people at the bar, all crowded around a flat screen, watching the news and talking about Chicago's shoot-out on the Drive. We found a table in a corner. Lawson told me I shouldn't drink with the meds they gave me. I thanked her for the advice and got a Fat Tire on draft. Lawson shook her head and ordered an Absolut with a twist. I took a deep draw on my pint and sat for a moment in the happy state of being alive. Lawson took a small sip and watched me.

"What did you find in the kayak?" I said.

"Short-barrel thirty-eight revolver. Recently fired."

"How about the rifle?"

"Nothing yet, but we'll find it. He had a key to the boathouse along the lagoon. We figure he shot you, then let himself in and grabbed the boat."

"And what? He was going to just paddle away."

Lawson shrugged. "Maybe. Tell you the truth, we weren't exactly looking for a guy in a kayak."

"Any ID?"

"We're running the prints now."

"And you think that's it?"

"Isn't it?"

"Who shot him, Lawson?"

She slipped her elbows onto the table and crowded forward in her seat. "I thought you might have an idea on that."

"You think it was me? Jesus Christ." My cell phone buzzed and I flipped it open. "Yeah?"

"Nice job, Kelly. Very nice job."

I held up a finger to Lawson and walked out the back door onto Cleveland Street. A drunk was sleeping in the cold. I watched him scratch himself as the mayor congratulated me for having the balls to play judge, jury, and executioner.

"You took care of things. Nice and simple. Took care of our city."

"Mr. Mayor—"

"It's something I don't forget, Kelly. Make no mistake about that."

"Mr. Mayor, I never fired my weapon."

"I understand, son."

"I drew down on him with my handgun, but I didn't fire."

"Say no more. We're on an open line here. Not a problem. Whatever happens, don't worry about it. No one's throwing a rope around your neck. You understand me? Where are you?"

"In a bar."

"By yourself? You want me to send someone down there to drink with you?"

"No, I'm with Agent Lawson."

"The FBI broad?"

I could sense the mayor's sex drive pop up from whatever dark place it slept, head moving, tongue flicking. Not a pleasant image in an already unpleasant conversation. But there it was.

"Yes, Mr. Mayor."

"Jesus, I'd like to throw a shot in her. You gonna throw a shot in her?"

I didn't respond. The mayor, of course, took that as acquiescence.

"You fucking Mick bastard. That's great. You deserve it. You really do. I can't say this publicly because of the tragedy on the Drive today, but you know what? It could have been worse. Much fucking worse. And I say that with all due respect and a heavy heart. You're a hero, Kelly. Nothing less. I gotta run. We're doing a press conference tonight. Listen, have a couple drinks on the city. Celebrate that piece of shit being dead. And, Kelly?"

"Yes, Mr. Mayor?"

"Stick it up her ass for me, will ya?" The mayor's voice cracked at the seams with sudden laughter, before bursting over into some sort of demented fucking chuckle. I cut the connection and headed back into the bar.

"The mayor sends his best."

"Does he?" Lawson said.

"Yeah, he's a real prince of a guy."

"He's disgusting."

"Well, there's that, too."

"He gave you the old pep talk, right? Make sure you nail the FBI broad, all that crap."

"We really need to talk about this?"

"You're right. No sexist pig is going to ruin our celebration." Lawson raised her glass. "Here's to Kelly. Taking care of the bad guys."

I shook my head. "My gun hasn't been fired, Lawson. You know that. So, what exactly did I shoot him with?"

She shrugged. "Don't know. But if you didn't shoot him, who did?"

"Exactly my point. If it wasn't one of your agents, it had to be a third party."

"And you're thinking of the accomplice?"

"Yes, I am."

"The accomplice no one believes exists."

"Is that what they're saying now?"

Lawson leaned forward and tapped the back of my hand. "That's what they've always been saying. Listen, putting this guy down is no big deal. He killed four people and critically injured another. And that was just on the Drive today. Between you and me, it's a blessing."

"I didn't shoot him, Lawson."

She leaned back and sighed. "Don't fuck up my case. It's all nice and neat. Wrapped up and put to bed."

"Not if there's an accomplice out there."

"There isn't."

"Then how did this guy get his head blown off?"

"You want to hear a theory?" she said.

"Love to."

"You shot him, then dumped the weapon in the lake. Why, I'm not sure. Well, no, I am sure. He wasn't an immediate threat to you and he was clearly going to be apprehended, so there was no way you could justify pulling the trigger legally."

"So I used a second weapon and then got rid of it."

"Gives you deniability when we have this conversation. Even a little insurance."

"And kills someone you and the mayor both wanted dead."

"Myself, the mayor. Everyone from here to Washington. For Chrissakes, Kelly, we talked about this."

"You talked about it, but it didn't happen that way. The trajectory of the bullet and angle of the wound will confirm it."

"Assuming any of those tests are done." Lawson nibbled at a pretzel and waited for me to see the light. Reality is relative, meaning it happened whatever way the Bureau says it happened.

"We'll be at the mayor's press conference tonight," she said, "then issue a statement tomorrow, confirming the dead guy was our shooter. He was killed by an unidentified law enforcement agent as he resisted arrest."

"You don't believe that," I said.

"I believe someone wants this to end, and that's fine with me. An accomplice turns up down the line, I've moved on and it's some other guy's problem."

"Look out for number one. Right, Lawson?"

"You were a cop in this town. You know how it works."

I lifted the pint to my lips and drained it. The cold beer felt good at the back of my throat and I rattled the empty glass on the table between us.

"You want another one?" I said.

She shook her head. "No. I had two last night."

"And?"

"Three drinks a week. That's the limit." She tugged a crumpled pack of cigarettes from her pocket and lit one up.

"Bartender's not gonna like that," I said.

Lawson slipped her shield onto the table. "I'm not a drunk, Kelly."

"I didn't say you were."

She blew smoke in a cool, blue stream over my head. "I don't even have a problem with it."

"Okay."

"Fuck you."

The bartender got a nudge from a patron. I could see him starting over to us. Then he caught a glimpse of the badge and retreated back behind the taps.

"Why don't you just tell me your story?" I said.

"What story?"

I spread my hands out, palms up.

Lawson let a smile slip. "Cops all have stories. Right?"

"I know I do," I said. "Hold on while I get a beer."

I went up to the front. The six people in the place now had an idea who we were and why we were in the area. I could feel their eyes on me as I waited for my pint. Finally, an old-timer at the elbow of the bar spoke up.

"You involved in that stuff down by the lake?"

His voice was full of smoke and whiskey. A doctor might call it a walking advertisement for emphysema. I found it comfortable.

"I was," I said.

The old-timer coughed up some phlegm and rapped his knuckles on wood. Then he sank into his drink. I had the bartender back him with a second and carried my pint to the table.

"The locals love us," I said.

Lawson glanced toward the taps. "Oh yeah?"

"Yeah." I took a sip on my fresh pint. "Now you gonna tell me your story?"

"It's nothing too spectacular." Lawson stared at whatever was left in the bottom of her glass as she spoke. "Been an agent for almost fifteen years. Divorced the last five. It was mostly my fault. I let the job eat me up, and Kevin got sick of being in a relationship by himself. Packed up one day and left. Took our little girl with him."

"He has custody?"

"The relationship was my fault, but the divorce was all him. At the time of the separation, Kevin knew I was heavy into one investigation and had two others in trial. I was putting in twelve-hour days and spending my nights working out the details for what we were going to do tomorrow."

"And you were drinking?"

Her eyes crept up to mine. "You know how it is. Strategy sessions over dinner, head to the bar afterward. You're working the whole time, but, yeah, there were a lot of late nights. Thing is, Kevin hired a PI to tail me."

I whistled. Lawson nodded.

"No kidding. He got me on tape at some places on Rush. Pulled the bar tabs. Stuff like that. His attorney sent me the whole package one night. Told me it was all going into a custody motion. They'd paint me as a drunk, whether I was or not."

"And you caved?"

"No choice. That kind of thing gets into a public hearing and the Bureau's done with you. Especially a woman. So I gave him what he wanted."

"How about your girl?"

"Her name's Melanie." Lawson's face puckered around the edges. She wanted that second drink now, but there was nothing for it. "I saw her once a month for the first couple of years. Then Kevin got remarried. They had their own child. Now I don't see her so much anymore. Sad thing is, I mind it less and less."

"I'm not sure I believe that."

Lawson tapped her fingers lightly on the table. "Thanks."

I took another sip of beer. "You ever wonder if it's worth it?"

"You ever wonder that when you carried a shield?"

I shook my head.

"Of course you didn't. Nobody ever does. The job is the job and always will be. Thing is to make sure you got your bases covered." Lawson shrugged. "I left myself vulnerable. I paid the price."

"And you don't plan on making that mistake again?"

Her eyes flashed for a moment, then went gray. She shook her head and rolled her empty glass between her palms.

"Do me a favor," I said.

"What?"

"Keep the door open. Just for a day or two."

Lawson looked up. "Why?"

"You said you thought there might be some other reason a killer would draw me into this case. Some other connection."

"I'm listening."

So I told her about the CTA crash at Lake and Wabash. Same spot on the L tracks, thirty years earlier to the day.

"Coincidence, Michael. And how does it tie into you?"

"I was on the train when it derailed."

Surprise flickered across her face. "You must have been just a kid."

"Nine years old. So you see, there's more 'coincidence' here than just a date on a calendar."

"I still don't see it." Lawson worried the edge of a bar napkin between her fingers. "I understand what you're saying, but I just don't see it."

"Let my guy finish taking a look."

"Herbert?"

"Hubert. Hubert Russell. Give him a day or two. If nothing turns up, you close the case and head on to bigger and better things."

"When are you meeting with him?"

"Tomorrow."

"You, Hubert, and Rodriguez, right?"

"Probably."

"What's up with Rodriguez, anyway?"

"What do you mean?"

"Never mind." Lawson pushed back from the table. "Thanks for listening, Michael."

"Like you said, we all have a story."

"I have to head downtown. Go home and get some sleep. You look like you need it."

"How about my angle?"

"I'll give you a day. If there's nothing there, you sign off on your statement and we all move on."

She left without another word. I looked over at the old-timer, still sitting at the elbow. He shrugged. I climbed up on the stool next to him and bought us each a shot of Wild Turkey. The old-timer told me Lawson was a fine-looking woman. I told him she probably was, but I had something finer. And I wasn't talking just about looks. The old-timer asked me what I was doing then, sitting there with him, drinking. I thought that was a good question and left the bar, feeling a little better about things and intent on tracking down my girl.

CHAPTER 29

I found Rachel inside an examining room at Northwestern Memorial. She was lying on a gurney and staring up
at the ceiling while another woman shone a light in her
eyes.

"They're green and they're gorgeous," I said.

The woman snapped off her light and was about to call
security when the judge intervened.

"Ignore him," Rachel said. "He's my boyfriend."

Trumpets didn't exactly sound as the last sentence rolled
off her tongue, and I thought I might have been better served
muttering non sequiturs with the old-timer at the bar.

"Family and friends are not allowed back here," the woman
with the light said. I glanced at her name tag: JAIME SINGER,
ATTENDING PHYSICIAN.

"Sorry," I said. "How long do you think she'll be?"

The apology seemed to buy me some rope. Jaime even
smiled as Rachel sat up.

"Actually, we're just about done." The doc turned to her
patient. "Your X-rays show no damage and it doesn't look like
you sustained any sort of concussion. The cut on your head

isn't deep enough for stitches, so we'll just stick with the butterflies. You still have a headache?"

Rachel shrugged. "It's getting better."

Jaime took out a pad of paper and began to scribble. "I'm going to give you something for the pain. Then maybe Lancelot here can give you a ride home."

Jaime and Rachel looked at me and laughed. I didn't get it, but that didn't seem to matter. Then Jaime was gone. And we were alone.

"You okay?" I said.

"A little sore, a little light-headed, but I'm fine. What are you doing down here?"

I shrugged. "Came to get you."

She sighed and held out her arms. I pulled her close.

"What happened at the lakefront?" she said.

"We can talk about it later."

Rachel nodded into my shoulder.

"I'm sorry, Rach."

She looked up. "For what?"

"This. What we talked about this morning. Everything."

She shook her head. "This wasn't what I was talking about. What happened to me today could have happened to anyone. In fact, it did happen to a whole bunch of other people. Except much worse. And none of them even knew you."

She was right, but that didn't touch the hollow inside, the fear that flared every time I saw the emptiness in Katherine Lawson's eyes and wondered when it might again be mine. I folded my arms around Rachel, trying to capture what lay between us, trying to keep it safe.

"I love you, Rach."

She drew me down and kissed me hard. "You better, pal. Now take me home. Hospitals give me the creeps."

We filled her prescription at the hospital pharmacy and caught a cab north. On the drive home, she tucked the top of her head against my cheek and immediately fell asleep. I sat quietly, listening to the cabbie talk on his cell and watching the headlights drift past.

CHAPTER 30

Nelson sat in a jet-black Chevy, engine idling, watching the front door to the graystone. He'd dumped the rifle he used to kill Robles in Lake Michigan. Then he'd slipped onto Lake Shore Drive, where he'd mingled with the bewildered, the bloody, and the freshly dead before disappearing into the neighborhood.

Now he pulled a long knife from a towel on his lap. His mind cast back to the day Robles told him about the black case and the lightbulbs. His dead friend had taken them because it was 1998 and it was just that easy. The army was giving him the shove, why not make them sweat a little? Robles didn't know exactly what the bulbs contained, just that he'd been given the job of guarding them, four hours a day, for three months inside a bioweapons lab at Maryland's Fort Detrick. That was enough for Nelson. He took the case from his friend. Then he did some digging, and turned up "Terror 2000."

Issued in 1998, the Pentagon's classified report outlined potential terrorist threats to the United States. Prominent among them was something called the "subway scenario": an attack involving the introduction of lightbulbs filled with weaponized anthrax into a major urban subway system.

The Pentagon was so concerned about such an attack, it authorized the lab at Fort Detrick to conduct experiments on its feasibility. The testing went on for five years, from 1993 through '97. According to "Terror 2000," some scientists loaded their lightbulbs with anthrax that had been genetically modified to be harmless. Others, however, insisted on the real thing for their tests. Nelson wasn't sure which brand of bulb his friend had lifted from the lab. He was rooting for the latter, but didn't really give a fuck. The lightbulbs were in place. When they fell, they fell. And Chicago would learn to live with the consequences.

Meanwhile, there were choices to be made and smaller, more personal bits of pain to inflict. A green and white Checker pulled up to the graystone. There were two people in the back, but only one got out. It was Kelly's judge. She had a bandage on her head and kept her gaze to the ground as she disappeared into her building. Nelson waited for the cab to pull away. Then he slipped the knife under his jacket, eased out of the car, and walked toward her front door.

CHAPTER 31

I directed the cab north. Rachel had invited me to stay at her place, but I knew the day would hit hard once she got inside. So I told her to sleep in and call me tomorrow. I needed some sleep myself. And my dog could use some dinner. Or maybe it was the other way around. Either way, a nightcap seemed like it might make everything go down a whole lot easier.

I slipped in the door of the Hidden Shamrock at a little before nine, pushed past a knot of people, and headed to the back room. There was a scattering of patrons at some tables and four or five more lounging on soft couches arranged around a fireplace that looked like a living room. I skipped all of that and headed for the bar. If I'm going to drink, I want to sit on a straight-backed chair with a row of heads on either side. If I want to sit on a soft couch, I go home. That's where soft couches belong.

A bartender I didn't recognize floated over and skidded a beer mat my way. "What will it be there, partner?"

He was an Irishman. That much I knew straight off. His hair was spiked blond with silver tips. He had a lightning bolt tattooed on his hand and danced a bit in his shoes as he stood.

"Give me a Booker's neat," I said.

"Booker's neat, over." He turned, grabbed a glass, and spun back to the bar. "So what's shaking there, sir? Out for a little, you know?"

Large blue eyes rimmed in red rolled to the left, toward a couple of women perched at the end of the bar.

"I know those two. Mama." He gave out a hoo-haw like Al Pacino in *Scent of a Woman*, dropped some whiskey into the glass, and pushed it my way. "If you want to be getting the ride, there's the ticket, boyo."

I took a sip and watched myself age in a bar mirror. The Irishman, apparently, required no response and kept talking.

"Name's Des. The right honorable Desmond Walsh."

I passed along my vitals.

"They're all talking about that shit this afternoon," Des said, lifting a foot and planting it alongside the speed rack.

"Lake Shore Drive?"

He nodded. "Couple of firemen came in. Told us it was an awful fucking wreck."

I sat some more with my drink.

"Heard they killed the cunt," Des said.

"Really?"

"Coppers blew the fucker's head off. Too good for him, you ask me."

"How do you know they got him?"

Des nodded toward a bank of TVs showing the Bulls game. "Mayor's gonna be on tonight. Give us the old play-by-play."

"Thank God for Mayor Wilson, hey?"

"Thank God for them coppers. That boy was never gonna see the inside of a cell. Not in this town."

A waitress beckoned and Des wiggled his way back down the bar. The Irishman was right. Chicago wanted some blood spilled and they didn't want to wait. Wilson understood that. So did Lawson. So did the media. They'd give people their dog-and-pony show and a head to stick on a pike. If I didn't want to partake, that was fine. But the show would go on.

I took another sip of whiskey and again considered the merits of the bar mirror on the wall. On one side of it was a charcoal sketch of Brendan Behan and an illustration of an Irish patriot I didn't recognize getting his neck stretched by the British. On the other side was a Blues Brothers poster and what looked like an old railway schedule in a cheap brown frame.

"Des."

The bartender was earnestly chatting up the waitress rather than pouring the drink she'd ordered. He grabbed the bottle of Booker's on his way back and topped me off. It was the third drink I'd seen him give away in ten minutes and I wondered, not for the first time, how the Shamrock kept its doors open.

"That picture." I nodded to the railway schedule. "Could I take a look?"

Des pulled the thing off the wall. "Wabash Railway, 1923." The Irishman looked up at me. "Don't know a fucking thing about it."

He laughed like a lunatic and made his way back to the waitress, giggling about the useless shit Yanks stick on walls. I took a closer look at the old schedule. What had caught my eye was the logo: WABASH RAILWAY in Old English script over a yellow background. Underneath it a black train belched smoke and steamed down a set of tracks. The design wasn't identical to the cardboard cutout someone had left on my doorstep, but it wasn't far off either. I flipped open my cell and punched in a number.

"Mr. Kelly, how are you?"

"Okay, Hubert. What's up?"

"The news is saying someone shot up Lake Shore Drive today. Then you guys shot and killed him."

"And you're thinking our case is solved?"

"Is it?"

"Keep going. There's at least two bad guys and only one of them is dead."

"You sure?"

"Yes, how's it going?"

"Slow. I got some data running on the current investigation. Checking everything against your personal history."

"What about Jim Doherty's files?"

"Just cracked them a few hours ago. Got some odds and ends popping up."

"Like what?"

"Nothing special."

"What do you have, Hubert?"

"Background stuff, mostly. Weird connections. For example, did you know there were two train crashes almost identical to yours? One in Des Moines in 1978. Another just outside St. Louis, three months before Chicago."

"Commuter crashes?"

"No, these were freight trains. No one hurt, but similar sorts of accidents, one train hitting a second and then accelerating after the initial collision."

"That is pretty random."

"There's more. Both of the freight train crashes were investigated by the NTSB. They determined that an engine-override device made by an old company called Transco malfunctioned, causing the first train to accelerate unexpectedly. In both cases the failure turned a minor incident into a major accident."

"I still don't see much of a connection to Chicago."

"Hang on," Hubert said. "I pulled the blueprints for the train you were riding in. They were in one of the files your friend Doherty gave us. The CTA had the same override device installed on your train."

"Made by Transco?"

"One and the same."

"No one ever connected the dots back to Chicago?"

"Doesn't look like it."

I took a sip of Booker's and thought about the CTA car bucking that night, the surges of power rumbling through a nine-year-old's sneakers.

"Transco no longer exists?" I said.

"Long gone."

"Who owned it back in the day?"

"It's pretty murky."

"I bet. Keep looking and remember what I told you. Think out of the box." I spun the framed photo of the railway schedule in a circle on the bar. "I got another random thing I want you to check out. The black-and-yellow logo I gave you . . ."

"I ran an image search through a couple of databases, but haven't gotten a hit yet."

"That's good, kid. Listen, I want you to look up an old outfit named Wabash Railway."

"Wabash?"

"Like the street. According to their press, they ran the world's longest electrified railroad back in the 1920s. From Toledo and Pittsburgh through Chicago to the Mississippi."

"What am I looking for?"

"Their design is the closest thing I've seen to the logo I gave you. I figure what the hell, maybe there's something there."

There was a pause, then Hubert's voice came back down the line. "Old English type and a black train over yellow, right?"

"You pulled it up on the Net?"

"Got it in front of me. You're right. It's close."

"Check out Wabash. See what they did, who they worked with. Maybe you find Transco somewhere in the mix."

"You got it, Mr. Kelly." A pause. "Can I ask a question?"

"Shoot."

"Does any of this tie into our shootings?"

"Not sure yet. But remember, that's not the only game in town."

"So keep digging?"

"Keep digging."

I clicked off, drained my glass of its bourbon, and threw some money on the bar. Channel 6 was breaking in with a special-report banner: THE MAYOR'S PRESS CONFERENCE, LIVE FROM CITY HALL. Cue the music. Call in the clowns. I pulled on my coat and left the bar. I had better things to do. Like feed my dog and get some sleep.

CHAPTER 32

The kettle began to hum, lightly at first, then a high-pitched, insistent whistle. Rachel Swenson walked into the kitchen, switching off the knob for the gas and running her hands across the counter toward the jar of tea bags. She didn't want to take the pills they'd given her unless she had to. A cup of tea and an early night in bed would do just fine. She reached for a mug in the cabinet and thought about Michael Kelly, unshaven, arms folded, gun on his hip, slouched in the doorway of the hospital's examining room like he owned the place, which, in his mind, he probably did. Michael could be rough around the edges, but he was warm, and he was real. She loved feeling safe when he held her, and despised the danger that gave breath to that need for protection. Rachel sighed, grabbed a mug, and turned back toward the stove. A cool breeze plucked at the back of her neck. The image of an open window flashed through her mind; a premonition tiptoed up her spine. She turned again and he was there, inside her home, closing a hand over her mouth and slipping a needle under her skin.

Somewhere far off, her mug crashed from counter to floor. Then she was looking up and he was over her. She saw the

146

edge of a knife and tried to speak, but the words tumbled away. Michael's face flashed through her mind again and she felt indescribably sad at what felt like his passing. Then she fell, too, amazingly far, until, finally, she was alone, hiding in the blinding white.

CABRINI-GREEN

CHAPTER 33

Rachel Swenson woke up in the dark, sitting on a cold floor with one wrist handcuffed to what she guessed was a pipe. She held up a hand in front of her, but couldn't see it. Then she listened. There was the sound of traffic, maybe a car horn, but it was distant, muffled. Closer, she could hear the drip of water. Finally, the scratch of a footstep. First one, followed by a second.

She felt along the ground for a weapon, but found nothing. So she balled her free hand into a fist and waited. The scratching stopped. She lifted her head. The breathing was quick and near. Something clicked, and light splashed onto her face. Then a hand covered her mouth. Another pinned her against the wall. She opened her eyes and saw a young black boy smiling back. Behind him, a second face surfaced. Not much older. He was smiling, too.

"You gonna scream, lady?" The first boy's voice was soft, an edge glittering underneath.

"She's all hooked up to the pipe." The second wrenched Rachel's shackled wrist. She winced, but didn't cry.

One of them slapped his hands against the walls while the other hopped around in front of her. She could almost see the thoughts speeding between them, the frenzy building. Two kids, about to step into their adult lives.

The second came close again and crouched.

"Don't," she said. He tore her blouse to the waist and punched her hard on the jaw. She hit her head against the wall and slumped awkwardly to the floor.

The first was on top of her, tearing at the rest of her clothes. Then he was gone, thrown into a corner by his friend. The dominant one would go first. His pants were already half undone. He pulled at his zipper and came closer. She was on her back, vision blurred in one eye and bleeding from the mouth.

"We gonna do what we do." The kid pointed behind him. "Both of us gonna hit it. So just let it be."

"No." She didn't know where that word came from or why. But she knew she was good with it.

The boy cocked his head and wrinkled his nose. "That what you want?"

She shook her head and didn't know what she meant. The boy disappeared for a moment. He returned holding a brick.

"You want to feel it or no?"

This time she opened her mouth to scream. The boy lifted his brick and the world went gray.

CHAPTER 34

"Maybe you did shoot him and you just don't know it."

"Fuck you, Rodriguez."

The detective grinned and kicked his feet up onto his desk. It was 6:30 in the morning and we were holed up inside Area 3 on Chicago's North Side. A recap of Mayor Wilson's press conference from the night before played on a TV in the corner. I looked idly for Katherine Lawson, but couldn't find her in the cluster of suck-ups standing behind His Honor.

"What do you want from me?" Rodriguez said and clasped his hands behind his head. "I don't know who killed the guy."

"Question is: Do you care?"

"It's the feds, Kelly. Besides, I got a stack of fresh murders piled up and getting colder by the minute." Rodriguez gestured toward the tube. "If the mayor says one of the good guys took him out, who am I to argue?"

"What else did you work up?" I said.

"Case is closed. Bad guy shot in the head."

"What did you find?"

Rodriguez sighed and pulled his feet to the floor. Then he opened up a file and slipped on a pair of glasses.

"When did you start wearing glasses?"

"Fuck off." He shoved a report under my nose. "Guy's name was Robert Robles. Chicago native. Born in a toilet at the old Greyhound station. Mom left him there for the cleaning crew."

"Not exactly the way you want to come into the world."

"No. DCFS bounced him all over the place. A few juvie offenses, but nothing too bad. Kid turned eighteen and decided he wanted to see the world. Two years in Somalia with the Eighty-second."

I flipped through his service record, lingering on Robles' photo, dress greens with beret cocked to one side, lips parted, eyes trying hard to make a killer into a soldier.

"Guy knew how to shoot," I said and turned the picture over.

"Yeah. He did another two years in the military when he got stateside. Looked like a lifer. Then he receives a general discharge. Not really sure why yet."

"And after he got out?"

"Don't know. He had no family that we know of. Work records show him in Seattle for six months, working a construction gig. Then he disappeared."

"Until he reappeared and started lighting up Chicago."

"Pretty much."

"I don't know this guy, Rodriguez."

"I sort of figured that."

"So why was he so interested in me?"

The detective shrugged.

"What else you got?" I said.

"We found his rifle, a Remington 700 just like the Loop shooting. He dumped it along with a camera and some other items in a duffel bag near the scene. Also got a trace on both weapons." Rodriguez pushed across another piece of paper. "Fifty 700s were clipped from a warehouse outside Hammond two weeks ago. These are the first two to surface."

"Meaning whoever lifted them might have forty-eight more," I said.

"Always the optimist, Kelly. Feds sent a team down there last night. The locals had a tip on a lukewarm suspect, but were sitting on it. Lawson suggested they expedite things."

Rodriguez turned over a picture. The man was middle-aged, maybe Russian, with a flat nose, heavy forehead, and black tongue hanging past his chin.

"They found this guy, strung up by a wire in his bedroom closet. Been there awhile."

"Robles didn't like a trail?"

"Apparently not."

"What else?" I said.

Rodriguez pulled out a second file.

"A maintenance worker found her yesterday morning, dumped alongside an auxiliary line of tracks in the subway."

I ticked open the folder and picked up a crime scene photo. The woman I'd seen wrapped in plastic was named Maria Jackson. She was black, early twenties, with her throat cut to the bone. I ran my eyes across the police report.

"We figure it's gotta be connected," Rodriguez said. "Coroner says she'd been dead six, eight hours."

I looked at the photo again. Cracked glass for eyes and the smile, wicked and deep, yawning just beneath her chin.

"So Robles, or his accomplice, cuts her throat somewhere else and dumps her."

"According to the feds, there is no accomplice," Rodriguez said.

I looked over the top of the file. "Who is she?"

Rodriguez turned up a booking photo of the victim, throat intact, body warm, blood still pumping nicely through her veins.

"Jackson was a working girl. Vice says she could usually be found on a corner near Cabrini-Green. What's left of it, anyway."

Rodriguez produced a street map of the area around Clinton and Congress.

"There's a parking lot under the highway, next to the Blue Line stop. City actually owns the property. CTA keeps a maintenance access door right here." Rodriguez tapped at the access door I already had a key to. "It's a half mile or so from the street to where the body was actually found, but that's the closest entry point to the subway."

"Forensics?"

"Our guys found trace evidence of blood on the door frame. Preliminary match to the victim."

"Anyone in the neighborhood see anything?"

"Bus station's a block away. Not exactly the best spot to pick up a reliable witness. Otherwise, the block's full of factories. We figure he dumped her at night. Place would have been like a ghost town."

Rodriguez flipped the files shut, put on his watch, and drained his coffee. "Course, none of this matters much. We got the guy who killed Maria Jackson. Or, rather, you got him." The detective smiled, cocked his finger, and shot me.

"What are you doing now?" I said.

"I'm about to get rid of you. Why?"

"I told Hubert Russell I'd meet him later this morning. He's been working the stuff I gave him."

"I just got some paper on him." Rodriguez picked through the pile on his desk.

"Hubert?"

"Kid was leaving a party in Boystown last week. Car followed him down the street. Couple of guys got out and pushed him into an alley."

"Tough guys, huh?" I began to read through the report Rodriguez had handed me.

"Witness said it was a green Camaro. Said they came out of the car with what might have been a baseball bat. Owner is an asshole named Larry Jennings. Been arrested twice on similar assaults."

"You guys get a tag number on the car?"

"Back of the initial report."

I turned the report over and saw the number, along with Jennings' phone and address on the Northwest Side.

"So why didn't you pull him in?" I said.

"Hubert wouldn't cooperate. Refused to ID his attackers. Claimed he tripped and fell on the way home that night. Hate Crimes guys said it's not unusual. Kid just doesn't want the hassle."

"Or his name in the paper."

Rodriguez shrugged. "Maybe."

I sighed and flipped the file shut. "Can I keep this?"

The detective waved his assent. "So what is the kid working on? Oh yeah, your train crash from the seventies."

"Eighties."

"Whatever."

"You want to take a ride over later. See what he's got?"

"We got time for breakfast?"

"I told him I'd swing by around ten."

Just then Rodriguez's phone rang. He picked it up and grunted. I walked out to get some coffee. When I returned, the detective was tugging at his tie.

"Got a visitor out front. Rita Alvarez."

"Who's that?"

"You read the papers, Kelly?"

"Sure."

Rodriguez smoothed out the lapels of his jacket. "She writes for the *Daily Herald*. Smart, tough."

"And I assume good-looking?"

"You assume correctly."

"Pretty early for a reporter. What does she want?"

"Don't know. Something about the case."

"Guess she doesn't realize it's closed either. Mind if I stick around?"

Rodriguez shrugged and led me down a small hallway, then through a maze of cubicles. On the way, I dialed Rachel's number.

"Damn."

"What's that?" Rodriguez said.

"Tried Rachel twice this morning."

"No answer?"

"No."

"It's barely seven. She's probably sleeping in. After yesterday, I can't blame her."

"Yeah, but she usually picks up the phone."

The detective stopped and turned. "You worried?"

"I just wish I'd stayed at her place last night."

"Why didn't you?"

"Stupid."

Rodriguez shook his head. "You don't take care, you gonna lose that woman. Come on, it's this way."

CHAPTER 35

Rachel lay at the bottom of a deep well, cool air flowing over her skin. She wanted nothing more than to rest, slip into the comfortable black that pressed down all around her. Then the darkness began to lighten. The low buzz above her became distinct sounds, voices. Rachel opened her eyes. The first thing she saw was the brick used to hit her, a foot from her head. Beyond that, the empty face of the boy who'd used the brick. He was lying on his side, eyes open, throat gashed. The boy blinked once, a bubble of saliva at the corner of his mouth, and issued a low groan as his lungs emptied. Then he was dead. Rachel inched back from the widening pool of communal blood. To her left was the boy's flashlight, throwing crazy shapes up on the walls. From the right came sounds of a struggle. Then another body hit the floor. It was the second boy, tumbling out of the shadows and smiling vacantly at her for a moment before a hand grabbed his shoulder and flipped him back into the darkness. The man who'd brought her to this place picked up the flashlight and shined it in her face.

"Greedy fuckers. Must have busted through the lock on the door."

He ran a hand across her flanks, much like he'd size up a dog at the pound, checking to see what was broken.

"Beat you up pretty good, huh?" He spit on the tiled floor and uncuffed her from the pipe. Then he moved to a corner of the room.

Rachel pulled the torn pieces of her clothing together and took inventory of the rest. The boy had hit her a glancing blow, knocking her silly, but not completely out. Her cheek felt crushed, her left eye didn't work very well, and the bones in her jaw rubbed together where they shouldn't. She tried to flex her left hand and realized she also had a couple of broken fingers. Then she glanced over at her would-be rapists, one with his jeans still partially undone. Just kids. Fuck that. If God ever gave her the chance and the man who sat in the corner ever gave her his knife, she'd kill them all over again.

"You okay?"

His voice was rough, but welcome. She nodded and tried to stand up. The room around her tipped and tilted. She dropped to the floor and emptied her stomach against the wall.

"Take your time." The man was inspecting a long, black rifle and spoke without looking at her.

She wiped gingerly at the blood on her face and realized she was crying. Then she huddled back near the radiator. The man was talking to her, but his voice seemed far away.

"You understand what I'm saying?" The man was close now. She shook her head.

"No matter." He crouched down and shackled her again to the pipe. Then he left the room and returned, carrying a video camera and a tripod.

"Got a schedule to keep, Rachel, so don't fuck with me."

She watched him set up the tripod and mount the camera. He knew her name and had let her see his face, which meant he was going to kill her, or expected to die himself. Or both. She tried to process that as he pulled the shade off a window, uncuffed her from the pipe and dragged her to a chair in the middle of the room. A thread of light wound its way into the apartment and, for the first time, she was able to get a larger sense of where she was. The door to the room she was in stood to her right. Behind her was a wall, with a huge hole in it, leading to a second room that dead-ended into a second wall. She had seen the holes before. Cops called them honeycombs, tunnels dug out by gangs and used to link apartments in CHA high-rises. There weren't that many public housing high-rises left standing in the city, and they were mostly abandoned. If that's where she was, there'd be no one close enough to hear her.

"We have to make a recording," the man said and moved the camera between her and the window. He shoved a piece of paper in front of her. "This is what you have to say. Play any games and you wind up like your pals over there. Do it right and you might get out of this room alive. Course a lot of that depends on your boyfriend."

For the first time she saw some emotion, a dance of light across pale blue eyes, then gone. The man turned his back on her and began to fiddle with the camera again. She looked at the watch on her wrist like it belonged to someone else. She was further amazed to discover it was still working and read 7:00 a.m. On cue, a church bell tolled out the hours. A lonesome siren picked up the note, its cry waxing and waning in the streets below. Over the man's shoulder, she could see Chicago's skyline sketched in subtle morning shades. And then she knew exactly where she was. It had to be.

"I think I'm going to be sick again," Rachel said, testing her jaw and finding she could talk.

The man turned back toward her. "Don't be," he said.

The siren was clearer now, harder and cold as it moved closer.

"If you want to do this, then hurry up," she said and hung her head low.

"Okay, we're ready." The man moved behind the camera. "Remember, say what's on the paper. Nothing else."

The red light flared just as the church bell was finishing, the siren moving in and out, looking for trouble in some other part of the neighborhood. Rachel put her hands on either side of her swollen face and rubbed her good eye gently. Then she looked into the camera. The man waited. Rachel gave it five more good seconds before she cast her gaze down and began to read from the paper.

CHAPTER 36

Rita Alvarez stood as we came in. The reporter shook hands with both of us, smiling brightly, but focusing mostly on the detective. Rodriguez answered the unasked question.

"This is Michael Kelly. He's a private investigator, attached to the task force. If it's all right with you, he's going to sit in."

Alvarez nodded. I didn't know the name, but I recognized the face. She'd been one of the media throng at the CTA shooting in the Loop. I'd thought she looked smart back then. Now I'd get to see if I was right.

"I know who Mr. Kelly is," Alvarez said. "And yes, by all means, I think it would be good for him to be here."

The three of us sat. We were in a small room used by cops to question suspects and potential witnesses. In Chicago, the questioning often continued until the latter became the former, so it all seemed to make sense. Alvarez had brought a slim buff-colored folder with her. She laid it down on the table and folded her hands over it as she spoke.

"Thanks for seeing me on such short notice. And so early in the morning."

Rodriguez didn't respond. Like any good cop looking to extract information, he'd let Alvarez do most of the talking.

"As I indicated on the phone, I have some matters I'd like to discuss in connection with the recent sniper shootings." The reporter dropped her eyes briefly to her folder, found nothing there, and looked back up. "I've come across some information that may be relevant to your case. I'm happy to share it with you before we go ahead and publish. In fact, I'd prefer to. But I'd like to get some assurances."

Alvarez waited. Rodriguez waited. I watched. Finally, Rodriguez spoke. "We're not in the business of giving assurances, Ms. Alvarez."

"Rita."

"Rita. I can get someone from County in here if you want. But if this is relevant evidence, I'd suggest—"

"Save it, Detective."

I smiled to myself. I liked Rita.

"If you don't want to talk, off the record, I leave and go with what I have. Then you can call in the state's attorney, subpoena me, or whatever else you want. But the information will be public . . ."

I shuffled my feet and shifted in my chair. Alvarez turned on cue.

"And we may not want that?" I said.

Alvarez let the question hang, then moved her attention back to the detective.

"What sort of assurances are we talking about?" Rodriguez said.

"I want an exclusive on this story. Inside the task force. Access to the key players. Any breaks in the investigation before the competition, and a full, exclusive debrief after the case is put to bed."

"The case is already closed," Rodriguez said.

"Maybe you should take a look at what I have before you go too far with that."

That brought a grimace from the detective and a reluctant nod of the head. "Let's see what you got."

Alvarez pulled a single sheet of paper out of her folder and slid it, facedown, across the table. Rodriguez left the item untouched for the moment.

"How many people know about whatever it is we have here?" the detective said.

"Myself and my managing editor know about the letter's contents. This is a copy. I have the original in a safe place, including the envelope it came in." Alvarez shrugged. "It showed up sometime yesterday. We learned about it last night. There's no stamp, no postmark, and we're not exactly sure how it was delivered. We used gloves once we realized what we had. Still, you're gonna get my prints and probably prints from the mailroom. At least."

Rodriguez turned over the page. It was just a few lines, printed in block letters.

RITA,

I DID SOUTHPORT AND THE OTHER. ME ALONE. USED A .40-CAL AND REM 700. HERE'S ANOTHER ONE, IF U NEED MORE CONVINCING.

FUCK THE MAYOR. FUCK THE FBI. CARDINALS HATS ARE NEXT. CITY TOO. NBC.

"I checked my notes and the wires," Alvarez said. "You guys never offered details on the weapons in any of the shootings. If this is all wrong, just tell me, and I'll write it off as a prank."

Rodriguez looked up from the letter. "What's 'another one' mean?"

Alvarez pulled out two more pieces of paper and pushed them over. "These came along with the letter."

The first page was a street map of the area near Clinton and Congress. The second was a duplicate of the subway map that had been left on my doorstep. The spot where Maria Jackson's body was found was marked with an x and the word BODY scrawled beside it in the same blue Magic Marker.

"Looks to me like a section of the subway," Alvarez said. "I'm sure the CTA can tell you exactly where to look."

The reporter read our faces and tried hard to keep the smile out of her voice. "Unless, of course, you guys already know everything I'm telling you."

Rodriguez pushed the pages over to me and leaned back in his chair. "Son of a bitch."

Now the reporter grinned for real. "I knew it."

Rodriguez tipped forward again. "We have our deal, Rita. Don't fuck with me on it."

"I came to you, Rodriguez."

"Yeah, well, don't get so fucking excited. Makes me nervous. Yes, the details on the weapons are correct."

"And the maps?"

The words came grudgingly. But they came. "We pulled a body from this location in the past twenty-four hours."

"Which means . . . ," Alvarez said.

"This guy has an accomplice," I said. "He's alive and he's not gonna just go away."

Rodriguez pulled the pages back over and took another look.

"The cardinals' hats and the city. Think he's talking about the archdiocese?"

I shrugged. "Probably."

"What about this last thing?" Rodriguez glanced at the reporter. "NBC?"

"We were thinking the NBC tower," Alvarez said.

Rodriguez nodded. "Targeting the TV station, maybe?"

"Could be something else," I said and moved over to a computer terminal in the corner.

Rodriguez and Alvarez looked over my shoulder as I Googled "NBC THREAT ACRONYM." It showed up as shorthand slang coined by the Department of Defense. NBC: nuclear, biological, and chemical. As in weapons.

Alvarez let loose a low whistle. "That works, too."

"I'm thinking we better get Lawson on the line," Rodriguez said. He picked up the phone, then put it down.

"What about her?" He pointed to Alvarez, who suddenly didn't seem so essential. The reporter pulled a Baggie from her purse. Inside it was an envelope and more sheets of paper.

"Let me guess, the originals?" Rodriguez said.

Alvarez nodded. "Might be able to get some prints. Maybe DNA off the seal."

"Gonna keep yourself relevant, huh, Rita? What else you got?"

"I'd like to think we're past that point, Detective."

Rodriguez was getting squeezed a little. Part of me thought he didn't half mind.

"Tell you what, we're gonna honor our deal. But for right now, we have to keep you somewhere close. Just not right here."

"The feds won't let me sit in?" she said.

"If we approach them about it this morning," Rodriguez said, "not a chance. Thing is, you're just gonna have to trust me."

"And what if I don't?"

"Then I put a set of cuffs on you and throw you in a room anyway."

"Fuck you, Detective." Alvarez pushed up from her chair, picking up her folder and the Baggie with the originals.

"Sit down, Rita."

Alvarez thought about it and sat. The detective pushed in a little closer. "I'm in this city for the long run. So are you. I'm also a straight shooter. You wouldn't be here otherwise. Work with me on this and you won't be sorry."

Alvarez glanced over, but knew better than to think she'd find anything in my face.

"I want a room with a phone."

Rodriguez shook his head. "No phone, Rita. No Internet. No e-mail. Not until we figure out what we're looking at."

"I want an update every hour. And I need to be able to file something for tomorrow."

The detective gave a short nod.

"Don't screw me, Rodriguez."

"I won't, Rita. Promise."

Then the reporter stormed out of the room and into solitary confinement. Sure, she caved. But she did it with a little bit of grit. In Chicago, that counted for a lot.

"WHERE'S THE REPORTER?" Katherine Lawson was floating on a computer screen in a sea of cyberblue. We had filled her in on Rita Alvarez and scanned a copy of the letter and maps to her desktop.

"We have her on ice," Rodriguez said.

"What about the letter itself?"

"The original's right here." Rodriguez held up the Baggie.

"Looks like it was hand-delivered to the paper, but no one seems to have gotten a look at the guy."

"Wonderful," Lawson said. "Forensics is coming over to pick up the originals. And we're going to need to talk to the archdiocese."

"So you think this is real?" Rodriguez said.

Lawson rubbed the heel of her palm into her forehead. "I don't know what to think, except that we're all gonna look like a bunch of assholes if this thing blows up."

She was thinking about the press conference last night—the case they had already taken credit for solving.

"I'm gonna need to talk to the mayor," Lawson said. "Maybe get him on the phone with the church."

"This morning?" Rodriguez said.

"Sooner, the better. Meanwhile, I need to take a minute here with Kelly."

Lawson waited until the door closed behind Rodriguez before speaking. "I'm sorry, Michael."

"For what?"

"Mouthing off in the bar last night. Bragging about a case I thought I could bury."

"Forget about it."

"I don't think so. It seems like you've had a better grasp of things every step of the way. How is that?"

"Lucky, I guess."

"You still meeting Hubert today?"

"Supposed to. Why?"

"I'd like you to run the contents of this letter by him. See what he comes up with."

"You sure?"

"Yes. And get me everything else he's got. Including the stuff on your old crash."

"You buying into that?"

"I'm buying into you being two steps ahead of the field. If the edge lies with Hubert, I'd like to use it, rather than apologize later for ignoring it."

"Fair enough," I said.

"Good. Now, what are your feelings on today?"

"You still have a relationship with the archdiocese?"

"I can handle them, if that's what you're asking."

"That's what I'm asking. Talk to the cardinal. Talk to the mayor. Use whatever pull you have to get into the churches and shut them down until you figure out if the threat is real. And . . ."

"And what?"

"And hope whatever this thing is, it hasn't already started."

CHAPTER 37

Hubert Russell lived in a studio on Division, just west of Damen. The neighborhood was jumping, with new restaurants and bars that actually smelled good. Most of that goodness, however, had yet to float up and into the hotbox apartments, crammed into ancient brownstones perched up and down the block.

"Nice place you got here," I said and put my foot down on a cockroach the size of a small sofa. The beast squirted out from under and looked up to see if that was my best shot. I put my heel into it until I heard a crack, then a snap. Score one for the good guys.

"It's a dump, Mr. Kelly. But it's all I can afford right now."

I settled on the edge of a kitchen chair. Hubert sat at his desk. A wooden fan hung from the ceiling. Between the two of us there was hardly room to take a breath.

"You read the letter I sent over?" I said.

Hubert nodded. "I might have something for you."

I pulled a little closer. Hubert had a monitor hooked up to his laptop. Beside the monitor was a bottle of pills. Pain medicine for the kid's face. I watched as Hubert began to open up documents.

"After you called, I started pulling emergency room admissions across the city. Then I ran that data through a program that sorts the information and looks for certain patterns. Actually there are twenty-seven different filters in this program—"

I cut in. "Hubert, we might have some shit going on here."

"Yeah, yeah. What did I find, right? Okay, in the past twelve hours there have been sixteen people admitted to ERs in the city, complaining of scorched red skin, blisters, and"—Hubert checked his computer—"weeping sores. Conditions range from serious but stable to critical."

"So what?"

"So this program also matches symptoms to the signatures of different types of potential threats. These patients, all of them, seem to fit the pattern of an emerging chemical weapons attack. Specifically, a mustard-based agent."

"Mustard gas?"

"Some version of that, yes. Then I expanded the parameters to twenty-four hours' worth of ER admissions. Picked up four more cases."

I stared at the data on the screen. "How sure are you about this?"

"I've had your letter less than an hour, Mr. Kelly."

"So you're guessing?"

"It's a little more than that."

"Print me out the patient list," I said.

Hubert hit a key, and a printer somewhere began to hum.

"What do you think?" Hubert said.

"What do I think? I think we might be fucked."

I picked up my cell and punched in Rodriguez's number. Hubert, however, wasn't done.

"I got a little more, Mr. Kelly."

I disconnected. "Go ahead."

"I pulled background on the twenty victims. Started with the hospital admittance forms and dug from there. Focused on any religious affiliations."

More lines of meaningless text and numbers flashed up on the screen. Hubert highlighted a line of data. "Eighteen of the twenty identified themselves as Catholic. Half of them are registered in Holy Name's parish."

A tingle ran down the back of my neck. "Where are the rest registered?"

Hubert waved a hand around the room. "All over. Still, it's interesting."

"The ones that aren't registered at Holy Name—where do they work?"

Hubert hit a few keys, and the information reshaped itself on his screen. "Eight of them work in the Loop or River North area. Here you go."

Hubert flashed up a map with Holy Name Cathedral at its center and small flags for each person's workplace. The longest distance was eight blocks.

"They could have walked there from work," I said, "which means seventeen of twenty have a possible connection to the cathedral."

Hubert nodded. "Looks like it."

I picked up my cell again and punched in the detective's number. Rodriguez picked up on the first ring.

"Yeah."

"It's me. What's going on?"

"Lawson and the mayor have been on the phone with the cardinal. Archdiocese wants us to sit on it until we have something solid."

"Not too worried about their parishioners, I take it?"

"It's called damage control, Kelly."

"Yeah, well, I got something that might get things moving."

"What's that?"

"Hubert's gonna send you some data. Shows a pattern of hospital admissions over the past day or so. Bottom line is, we have twenty cases of what might be mustard agent exposure. Seventeen with connections to Holy Name Cathedral."

"What sort of connections?"

"The sort that makes me think you got a hot spot, Detective."

"Holy Name, huh?"

"It fits, Vince. Remember the letter referred to the cardinals' hats? Holy Name has the hats of Chicago's dead cardinals hanging from the ceiling."

There was silence, then a sigh. "Fuck me. Send over the data, and I'll get a team down there. Hold on." Rodriguez paused, then came back on the line. "Lawson wants everything the kid's got sent to her computer. And she means everything, Kelly."

Hubert tapped me on the shoulder and flipped his monitor around so I could see the screen of text he had pulled up. I nodded and continued talking to the detective.

"Not a problem. Just one more favor to ask." Then I told him what I needed.

"Why don't we let the feds handle that?" Rodriguez said.

"Because I'm concerned the feds will roll over and play dead."

"And you're going to go in there and bust balls."

"I'm going to go in there and explain the situation. Then I'm going to get the information I need."

Rodriguez didn't like it, but finally agreed to make the call. "Just don't piss this guy off."

"Why would I do that?"

"Yeah, right. Head down that way and I'll call you back."

I hung up. The text Hubert had accessed still glowed on his screen. It was a newspaper article. Page 3 from yesterday's *Trib*. The headline read: CHICAGO ARCHDIOCESE SETTLES SEX CASES FOR $12.3 MILLION.

Hubert watched as I read, then offered up one word. "Motive."

"Maybe." I slipped my cell back in my pocket and picked up my coat. "I gotta go. Send everything you have to Lawson's computer. Include whatever you found on the old train crash. Then just hang tight." I looked around the flat. "You okay here?"

Hubert nodded. "I'm good."

"You're a little better than good, Hubert. You sniffed out what might be a chemical weapons attack against the city and gave us our best lead on this guy."

"Guess that was pretty cool, huh?"

"Bet your ass. Keep it up. We're getting close to something. I'll call you in a couple of hours."

And then I left the kid, alone in his apartment, tapping away at a mountain of information, fishing for a shark in little more than a rowboat.

CHAPTER 38

It's called the House of 19 Chimneys. I thought about trying to count them, but didn't want to besmirch the romance of the place with anything as ordinary as fact. Instead, I got out of my car and walked a complicated path to the cardinal's doorstep on North State Parkway.

It had taken a couple of hours, but Rodriguez finally angled me the invite—not entirely surprising given the church's desperate need to put a lid on whatever was brewing inside their whitewashed walls. I was about to lift a heavy brass knocker when my cell phone buzzed. I stepped back to the sidewalk. It was Rodriguez again.

"You in yet?"

"On the precipice."

"We just ran some field tests at Holy Name."

"That was quick."

"Our guys kept things quiet and went in as a cleaning crew. Got a preliminary positive for some sort of mustard agent. Fucker spiked the holy water."

I wasn't surprised, but still felt a chill. Strange days, indeed.

"Does the archdiocese know?" I said.

"Not yet. Lawson's got the cisterns sealed off and wants to run some more tests first, so keep it to yourself."

"Fine."

"You really think our guy's an abuse victim?"

I looked up at the residence, swore I saw a curtain twitch, and, for just a moment, was back on the South Side. "I think it's worth a conversation."

"Guess it can't hurt."

"What about the press?" I said.

"What about them? They don't know a thing about the letter or Holy Name."

"What about Alvarez?"

"She'll be our mouthpiece. We get the story out the way we want, when we want. And she gets her exclusive."

"So you got that handled?"

"You worry about the cardinal, Kelly. Let me worry about Alvarez. Call me when you get done."

"Okay."

"And, Kelly . . ."

"What?"

"Don't be an asshole."

I cut the line and walked back up the cardinal's path. This time I picked up the brass knocker just as the door swung open. On the other side was a nun, dressed entirely in white and looking at me like she knew better. Behind her were three more nuns, hands tucked into their starched sleeves, faces cast in perpetual shade. The nun at the front door stepped aside without a word, and I walked in. The head of Chicago's two million Catholics swept around a corner with a smile and a handshake.

"Mr. Kelly."

Even at seventy-three years old, Giovanni Cardinal Gianni was still a bit of a rock star. On his seventieth birthday, *Newsweek* had dubbed the sturdy dark Italian "America's Own Pope." I wasn't sure how well that went over in Rome, but Gianni was here, smiling and, best I could tell, still in one piece. He ushered me into what I guessed to be a study and gestured to an armchair wrapped in velvet. "Please, sit down."

Like most Chicagoans, I'd driven by the cardinal's residence and wondered what the elegant pile of red brick and sandstone might look like inside. It was about what I'd thought. Floors of polished wood interrupted by hallways of polished marble. Large rooms cluttered with furniture no one used and pictures of saints no one knew. Bunches of flowers, bloodred and bone white, lurking in distant corners and sucking all the air out of the place. To my left and right, walls of books. Most of them, I was betting, Bibles.

"Can I get you some coffee, Mr. Kelly?"

"Thanks, Your Eminence. That would be nice."

Gianni raised a finger without turning his head. Somewhere behind him I heard some movement. A nun, I guessed, in search of a cup of joe. "We've already served lunch. But if you're hungry, I'm sure the sisters would be happy . . ."

"No thanks," I said. Gianni nodded and waited, one leg crossed over the other, dark face loose and relaxed, entirely empty of any sort of clue.

"I suppose you're wondering why I'm here?" I said.

Gianni spread his hands, palms up. "I spent most of the morning on the phone with the mayor and the FBI. They ask me to spend my afternoon with you, who am I to refuse?"

The cardinal's stick-on smile mirrored my own. He got up and walked to a picture window that looked out over a half acre's worth of bare trees and front lawn.

"So much for keeping things under wraps," the cardinal said. I followed his gaze out the window. A TV truck had just pulled up in front of the mansion. A camera crew scrambled out and began to shoot pictures. So much, also, for Rita Alvarez's exclusive.

"You know this town, Your Eminence. There's very little that remains secret for very long."

"We're not asking anyone to keep secrets, Mr. Kelly. Just a little discretion."

Gianni had been a rugby player in his day. I could see the game in the heft of his shoulders and the small, rough scars around his eyes when he scowled.

"So what happens next?" the cardinal said.

"We're checking out Holy Name, as we speak. Depending on what we find there, we'll develop a plan to sweep the rest of your churches."

"You know how many parishes there are in the archdiocese?"

I shook my head.

"Three hundred fifty-nine. You're going to check them all?"

"I don't know, Father. But we'll try to keep disruption to a minimum."

Gianni's laughter stopped just short of derision. "We're not a business, Mr. Kelly. People look at their church as a sanctuary. A place where they feel safe."

"Yeah."

The cardinal circled away from the window. "Not a fan of the church?" His Eminence could smell the lapsed Catholic in me clear across the room.

"All due respect, Father, how safe were the parishioners at Holy Name this week? How safe would they have been next week if we'd kept a lid on this thing?"

A moving statue of a nun emerged from the mists, carrying a silver service of coffee and momentarily saving me from eternal damnation. Gianni sat back down and poured us each a cup. The nun disappeared from whence she came.

"What is it I can help you with, Mr. Kelly?"

I took a deep breath and dug into it. "We'd like some information. About some of the sexual abuse claims from the past."

Gianni ran a thumb across his lower lip. "Go ahead."

"It's a natural line of inquiry, Your Eminence. Someone takes their revenge on the church for a wrong that was done to them as a child."

The cardinal looked past my shoulder, at his church's version of original sin, a history for which there was no simple act of atonement. No easy way to erase the stain.

"I understand the logic behind your query. All too well. Do you have a suspect?"

"No."

"Would you tell me if you did?"

"Maybe."

"And you think this spate of violence might be specifically tied to the abuse scandal?"

"At this point, Father, it's just a theory."

"I see." The cardinal sat back and fixed up his coffee with cream and sugar. Then he took a sip and continued. "As you know, our policy is clear. None of the archdiocese files are to be made public, save that which has already been revealed pursuant to a court order or negotiated agreement. If we feel there's an ongoing danger, we will contact the authorities with information. If the police have an identified suspect, we will also cooperate with respect to that specific person. Unfortunately, what you are suggesting is more like a fishing expedition. And, if I understand your request, might involve revealing the names of possible victims."

"You asked if I was Catholic before. At least that's what I got out of it."

"Yes."

"I haven't willingly stepped foot inside a church for ten-plus years. Want to know why?"

The cardinal's features tightened and the fingers of one hand rolled against the rub on the arm of his chair.

"Certainly, Mr. Kelly."

"I don't believe in your church. What was once my church. I think it's more an institution than a church. One that is out of touch with its people. One that likes to make up rules and hide behind them."

"Those rules, as you call them, are the bedrock upon which the church is founded. Without them, we would have no anchor to keep us steady, no foundation upon which to build. As the waters got deeper, the currents faster, as the ground beneath us began to shift its shape, we would find that, without those rules, we would have no faith at all."

As Gianni spoke, I felt the familiar sting of childhood, the lash of Catholic arrogance. It was palpable in the soft flow of words and dismissive tone. This was not a discussion between equals. It was a lecture. One steeped in beneficence and understanding, but a lecture all the same. Except I wasn't ten years old anymore, and I wasn't in the mood.

"All due respect, Your Eminence, but if those are the same rules that tell a woman she doesn't have what it takes to be a priest, or asks men who have never been married to counsel a couple considering the same, I have a problem with that."

"Those are doctrinal matters, Mr. Kelly."

"And the inherent evils of the condom, Your Eminence?"

The cardinal started to get up. "I suspect we have taken this as far as is practical, Mr. Kelly."

An image floated through my mind—Rodriguez counting the many ways I could be an asshole. I needed to play another card, and quickly.

"You know, Father, when I was a kid, I remember learning about something called the seamless garment of life."

The reference bought me a moment's pause. His Eminence lowered himself back into his seat. I kept talking.

"The idea was to accord life the highest value in any moral argument, in determining what is fundamentally right and wrong. If you made life the trump card in ordering your priorities, you would find it to be an unerring compass, one that would always lead you down the right path."

Gianni's dark lashes fluttered. "I'm familiar with the concept, Mr. Kelly."

"You helped to champion it, Your Eminence. It was the first major plank in your career as a theologian."

Gianni waited.

"Life is what's at stake here, Father. We're talking about real people dying. Potentially, a lot of people. But the number isn't even important, is it? If there's even one life at risk, that life must be weighed against your rules concerning the privacy of any records. And that life must prevail. Isn't that the calculus I'm asking you to make?"

Gianni tilted his head and looked at me as if I'd just walked into the room. "You studied under the Jesuits?"

"Maybe."

The cardinal laughed. "I knew it. Very well, Mr. Kelly. The church will help if it can. But we must use tremendous discretion in handling these records."

"Discretion's my middle name, Father."

Gianni made a gesture I assumed to be hopeful. We both stood up and began to walk.

"Maybe we can talk specifics once we have a handle on the threat?" I said.

"And when might that be?"

"I'd hope by day's end."

The cardinal stopped. "But you suspect this man *is* targeting the archdiocese because of the abuse scandal?"

"I said the scandal was a logical avenue to pursue, Father."

"But not a theory you necessarily subscribe to?"

"I don't subscribe to any single theory right now. This man is attacking the entire city, not just the church. And I think there is more at play here than we know. Maybe a lot more."

Gianni looked at me closely, but didn't respond. I glanced out the window. There were now three news vans and two live trucks parked outside the mansion.

"Maybe I could sneak out a side entrance?" I said.

The cardinal raised his eyebrows. "If only we all had it so easy, Mr. Kelly."

He led me to a service door that backed out onto an alley. I walked around to the front and found my car a half block down the street. My cell phone buzzed just as I slipped inside.

"Hubert, what do you have?"

"Where are you?" The kid seemed a little breathless.

"Just left the cardinal's residence. Why?"

"I took a closer look at the maps and letter you sent me. Then I talked to Detective Rodriguez and got a little more information on the originals."

"What's up, Hubert?"

"The street map this guy sent to the reporter. It was downloaded from MapQuest."

"So what?"

"I got a couple of pals who do a lot of work with them. MapQuest logs all its location requests, keeps records of all the computer IP addresses."

"In English?"

"The map sent to the *Daily Herald* was requested by a computer located at 1555 North State Parkway."

I glanced up as the massive front door to the mansion creaked open and stopped.

"You're telling me that map came from the cardinal's residence?"

"I'm telling you that's what MapQuest's records show."

"What do you think?"

"The guy we're dealing with is too sharp to make that mistake. I think it's a setup. Someone routed their request through the cardinal's IP address."

"Which means someone's sending us a message. I gotta go, Hubert."

I clicked off and scanned the block, looking for a shooter. The door to the residence swung open the rest of the way. Giovanni Cardinal Gianni stepped out onto a small portico and spread his arms wide. Cameras jockeyed for position and the elite of Chicago's media boiled at Gianni's feet.

I scanned a second time. Then I reached for the door handle. That's when the cell phone rang, except this time it wasn't my phone. And the ringing was coming from underneath my front seat.

CHAPTER 39

I found a prepaid unit taped under the driver's seat. It lit up red and blue in my hand every time it buzzed, almost like the thing was laughing at me, which it probably was.

"Yeah."

"Funny how things work, isn't it?"

I felt a ball of ice form in my stomach and a flicker somewhere deep inside my brain. "What do you want?"

"Look at the cardinal. Bloody great fucking hypocrite."

My eyes slid over to the mansion. Gianni was still on the front stoop, trying to hold the media hounds at bay. I thought the cardinal looked a bit chagrined. I wondered if he had any divine inkling as to just how bad his day might become.

"Want to see him executed, Kelly?" The electronic voice purred over the line. "Just say the word."

I searched one more time. Lawns, tree line, cars. Then I opened the car door.

"No," the voice said.

I froze, eased the door shut, and leaned back against the seat.

"Cardinal doesn't die today, Kelly. So let's drive. West

toward the Kennedy. And no fucking around. That is, unless you do want to see a bullet in him."

I turned the engine over, gripped the wheel, and headed toward the highway.

"I was worried you might not find the phone."

"My lucky day," I said.

"The camera is taped to your door seam, by the floor on the passenger's side."

I glanced over and saw the thin run of wire and a pinhole lens staring at me. I pulled the camera free and threw it into the backseat.

"Know what life's about, Kelly?"

"Why don't we cut the bullshit and boil this thing down."

"Is that the way you want it?"

"That's exactly how I want it. Leave everyone else out. City, church, feds, everyone."

"Underneath the other seat you'll find a flash drive. Play it and then see how you feel."

The line disconnected. I pulled down a dead-end street, popped my flashers, and reached under the passenger's seat. The flash drive was black with a piece of masking tape on it. A single word was written on the tape: RACHEL.

CHAPTER 40

Someone is going to die.

I sat in my car and felt that certainty pump through my veins. I took a minute to distill the violence into a more refined form and tucked it away until I needed it. Then I watched the video recorded on the flash drive a second time. Then a third. I picked up my cell phone and tried to call Jim Doherty. No answer. I clicked off and called Hubert. His voice mail picked up. My phone indicated a second call was coming in. It was Rodriguez.

"You done with Gianni?"

"He's got Rachel."

"Hold on a second." There was a pause and Rodriguez came back on the line. "Go ahead."

"He planted a cell phone in my car. Called to tell me about a flash drive he had planted there as well. She's on it, Vince. Some sort of video. Looks like she's beat up pretty bad."

"You never talked to her this morning?"

"No. She was reading from a script this guy wrote. Said I needed to do exactly as he instructed. Then she read off two addresses. One was Hubert's. The other was Jim Doherty's."

"The cop who gave you the old files?"

"Yeah. Said I should pick one and not worry about the other."

"You get hold of the kid?"

"No. Hold on, I got another call." I clicked over to the other line.

"Mr. Kelly, you called me?"

"Hubert, fuck yes, I called you."

"Sorry, I was just hashing through the rest of this material on the crash."

"Hubert, I need you to listen to me."

The kid shut up.

"I just got a message from this guy. He dropped two addresses we should assume are targets. One was yours."

I waited. "Hubert, you there?"

"You told me to listen."

"I'm gonna have them send a team over to your apartment, but it might be a while. For right now, I need you to lock your door, and don't let anyone in. No one. Unless it's me or some-one with a badge. You got it?"

"Yes."

"You have a weapon in the house?"

"What does that mean?"

"Just what I said."

"I have a steak knife."

"Get it. Lock the door and get the knife. Stay in the house and you'll be fine."

"This guy is probably playing us, Mr. Kelly. He likes to do that."

"Stay in the house, Hubert. Wait for the cops."

"Right. But, listen, I dug up some more interesting stuff . . ."

"I can't right now. Put it all on a disk or something and send it to me. But stay in the house until the badge gets there. Okay?"

"Okay, Mr. Kelly."

"Good kid. I'll talk to you . . ."

I clicked off and got back on the line with Rodriguez.

"Vince, that was Hubert. He's okay."

"I'll get someone over there."

"Not yet. This guy realizes I'm headed to the cops and maybe he starts killing people."

"He's already killing people, Kelly."

"There's a way to play this. But it's gotta be just me and you."

"What are we gonna do?"

"We're gonna find Rachel."

CHAPTER 41

Ifidgeted in the back booth of a carryout place called China Doll while Rodriguez watched images flash across my laptop. Rachel, bruised and beaten, staring into the camera, her eyes telling me where she was, her heart wondering when I was going to come get her.

"What are you thinking?" the detective said after he'd finished.

"I told Hubert to lock his doors and sit tight."

"What about Doherty?"

"Tried his cell and home. No answer."

"You thinking he's the target?"

I nodded.

"I can get a squad down there in ten minutes," Rodriguez said.

"If Jim's not dead already, anything other than me showing up alone will likely kill him. And Rachel along with it." I nodded to the video. "On the other hand, our guy's not expecting this."

"What are you talking about?"

I cued up the footage and played it from the top. Rachel's

face came into focus, her hands cupping her chin and partially obscuring her face.

"See that," I said and stopped the video.

"See what?"

"She doesn't start speaking right away."

"So what?"

"Listen to what's going on in the background."

I hit PLAY. First there was nothing but her breathing. Then the echo of a church bell tolling.

"Now look at her hands," I said. "She's showing us the face of her watch."

Rodriguez took a closer look at the digital readout. "Seven a.m. I'll be damned."

"Smart girl," I said. "And that's not all."

I hit PLAY again. Rachel started to speak. Underneath her words, a siren ebbed and flowed, sometimes getting closer, then moving away, then coming very close so she had to raise her voice to be heard. Rodriguez glanced across the table.

"That's a fire engine," he said. I nodded.

Rodriguez got on his cell phone. Five minutes later, he had a list. And we had some options.

"I took a ten-minute time frame for this morning," the detective said. "Centered it around seven." He showed me his list. "There were three firehouse calls. One in the Loop. One on the Northwest Side and one on the Near North."

I put my finger on the third address. "This one's three blocks from Cabrini."

Rodriguez nodded. "Maria Jackson was grabbed there. Let me see that video again."

He double-speeded through it until he found the image he

wanted. It was a wider shot, revealing a piece of the room behind Rachel.

"The wall behind her." Rodriguez pointed to a section of crumbling drywall. "At the very edge of the frame, you can just see the hole."

I looked closely. The detective was right.

"Tunnels," I said. "You thinking high-rise?"

"If it is, there's only one left standing in Cabrini."

I knew we should call for backup. I knew we should coordinate with the task force. I also knew Rachel was maybe less than a mile away. "Give me an hour before you call in the troops."

Rodriguez shook his head. "Fucking Kelly. Let's go before I change my mind."

"You sure?"

"Yeah, I'm sure. How do we play it once we get inside?"

"If he's there, he dies."

"That's what I figured." Rodriguez pulled out a snub-nosed revolver and laid it on the table. "Just in case."

I slipped on a pair of leather gloves. Then I picked up the gun and put it in my pocket.

"Let's go."

CHAPTER 42

The building sat fifteen stories high on an otherwise empty lot near the corner of Division and Halsted. Its outer porches were covered over in steel mesh, its pale concrete skin stitched with graffiti. The lower floors were boarded up, while the top two featured large black holes where windows once stood.

Rodriguez and I approached along Division. A couple of kids watched from a breezeway across the street and then melted into a two-story low-rise.

"Gangs usually tunnel between apartments on the top two or three floors," Rodriguez said. "I'm thinking we start there and work down."

"This place supposed to be empty?" I said.

The detective shrugged. "Don't count on it."

We came up on a back entrance. The plywood that covered it over had been pried loose, and we slipped inside. Dim light and a current of warm air greeted us. The high-rise might have been a shell, but the city was still heating it and providing electricity. We picked our way through the lobby, sectioned off with scratched Plexiglas. Metal mailboxes scored with bullet holes ran along one wall, and the linoleum floor was covered with broken glass and a handful of syringes.

Rodriguez motioned up and took the lead. We climbed the staircase in single file, guns drawn. An elevator door stood open next to the fourth-floor stairwell. I glanced down into the black hole. A set of eyes looked back.

"What the fuck?" A head popped up from the hole, hands already behind his head, gaze fixed on the barrel of my gun. "You guys five-oh?"

Rodriguez pulled the young man out of the shaft and shoved him up against the wall. The kid was maybe fifteen and held a narrow, angled head atop a precariously long neck. He wore loose baggy jeans and an oversize Chicago Bulls jacket.

"What's your name?" Rodriguez said.

"Chubby. You five-oh?"

"Shut up." Rodriguez took out a small flashlight and shined it into the shaft. All eighty-five pounds of Chubby had been sitting, or maybe sleeping, on the top of the elevator car that sat just a few feet below us.

"How long you been here?" I said.

"I come in once, maybe twice a week. Get warm. Sleep a little."

"You seen anyone around?" I said.

"What you mean by 'anyone'?" Chubby's voice rose at the prospect of perhaps having a card to play.

"A guy who doesn't belong," I said. "And a woman."

Chubby shook his head. "No woman. Seen a white dude. Maybe yesterday. Don't think he saw me, but he was coming from upstairs."

"You get a look at the guy?" I said.

Chubby smiled. "White dudes all look the same to me."

Rodriguez grabbed the kid by the collar. I glanced at the detective, who let the kid go. Chubby stepped back and watched both of us closely.

"You know which floor the white guy might have been coming from?" I said.

"I'd say top floor. No one else up there for sure."

"Why's that?" Rodriguez said.

"No wood on the windows. No heat. Colder than shit up there."

Rodriguez jerked his head toward the stairs. "I need you to go down into the lobby and wait. You're not there when I come down, I come looking for you. And that ain't good."

Chubby glanced back toward the elevator shaft. "I got some shit down there."

"Forget it," Rodriguez said. "Now get the fuck out of here before I lock you up."

Chubby didn't care about his stuff. Chubby also wasn't moving. "You slick boys goin' upstairs, best take me with you. I know how it works."

"How what works?" I said.

"The layout. Nigger can shift right down the hallway for you. See if your boy's there and tell you exactly where. Now, how much that worth?"

I put my gun to his nose, and Chubby's grin fell apart at the seams.

"You want to help?" I said.

Chubby kept his eyes on the gun. I took that as a yes.

"Do just what we say and don't say a word unless we ask you a question. You got it?"

Chubby nodded.

"Okay," I said. "Get behind us and follow."

And so we began to climb again, traveling on the edge of

Dante's circles—also known as Chicago public housing. Twice we heard a groan, once a thick whisper and some quick footsteps. Each time, Chubby slipped away, only to return with a nod to keep climbing. Eleven flights later, we hit the top.

"This is it," Chubby said, hunched in the stairwell. "No heat up here. Only safe place for a white man."

I edged my head around the corner and took a look down the corridor. Our guide was right. The wind was whistling through blown-out windows, dropping the temperature to whatever it was outside. I could only see two units on my left. Neither had doors on them. I ducked back into the stairwell.

"Any of the apartments up here have doors," I said.

Chubby shook his head. "Not likely."

"You think you could take a look for us?" Rodriguez said.

"Sure."

"Go ahead," I said. "Just walk down the hall and right back. Nice and slow. We'll be watching."

I stepped back and motioned with my gun. Chubby eased past us and around the corner. Thirty seconds later, he was back.

"Know exactly where your boy is."

I felt my heart jump and my fingers itch.

"How so?" Rodriguez said.

"Last apartment on the right," Chubby said. "Got a door and maybe a lock on it. Gotta be your boy."

"That unit tunneled out?" I said.

"They all got tunnels up here," Chubby said.

"Stay here," Rodriguez said.

I crept around the corner and moved down the hallway, the detective on my shoulder. Chubby was right. None of the units had doors, until we got to the last. We stacked on either

side. I took a deep breath and nodded. Rodriguez raised his boot
and kicked in the door. I went first, ducking low and scooting
along the wall. It was warmer in here, fetid, with fractures of
light cutting up the floor. I saw a shape and moved toward it.
Somewhere behind me, Rodriguez yelled "Police." I was turning over a body and staring down at a young black man, eyes
open, dead. There was a second boy close by. I took off my
glove and felt for a pulse. Blood greased my fingers as Rodriguez ripped the shade off a window covered over in plastic.
The apartment's north wall had been boarded up, sealing the
unit off from the rest of the floor. The opposite wall had a huge
hole in it. Rodriguez ducked through it and popped back out.

"Bedroom. Clear."

An empty chair sat in the middle of the main room. A second interior door stood ajar to my left. Rodriguez eased the
door open with his foot and ducked in.

"He must have moved her." The detective's voice drifted
back through the unit. I was staring at the chair Rachel had
sat in just a few short hours ago.

"Kelly, you hear me?"

I kicked the chair across the room. "I heard you. He knew
Rachel had tipped me on the video. Knew I'd come here."

"Couldn't have taken her too far," Rodriguez said and
paused. "Kelly, come in here."

I walked into the third room. Rodriguez had his back to me
and was running his flashlight over what looked like a bed. I
moved up behind him and felt my throat tighten. The mat-
tress was stained with blood.

"Looks like those stains have been here awhile," Rodriguez
said. "There's more on the floor. I'm thinking Maria Jackson."

The detective turned toward me. He held a buff-colored
envelope between his fingers.

"What's that?" I said.

"It was taped to the wall over the bed. Got your name on it."

I turned the envelope over. There was my name in block letters. Inside was a single photo. It was an old shot. Denny McNabb wore a White Sox hat and Peg had what looked like a can of Old Style in her hand.

"Who are they?" Rodriguez said.

"Jim Doherty's neighbors."

"Someone's playing games."

"Yeah."

Rodriguez sighed and kicked at some stray glass on the floor. I slid down against the wall and studied the photo.

"I can't keep a lid on this much longer," Rodriguez said. "Not with the bodies next door."

"Bring Lawson in now."

"You sure?"

I looked down at my cell. The text message light was blinking. It was from Hubert Russell.

"Yeah. Have her get a team in here. Get someone over to pick up Hubert as well. Tell Lawson I need two hours. Then they can move on the South Side."

"You think she'll go along?"

"She wants this guy dead. And she wants it off the books. I'm betting she gives me the window."

"What about Rachel?"

I wasn't going to ride to her rescue. At least not the way I'd planned. Instead, it was gonna have to be his way.

"I'm thinking you take Chubby and work the neighborhood. If this guy moved her, it had to be today. Maybe someone saw something."

Rodriguez crouched down so our eyes were level. "Two

hours. Then we come. And remember, don't wait on this prick. You get a shot, take it."

The detective straightened and walked into the other room. I could hear him on his cell, making his first calls, cranking up the logistics on a team for Cabrini. I needed to get going. Instead, I flipped open my cell and clicked on the first of Hubert's texts. The message was one line:

HANG ON TO THIS. MORE TO COME, INCLUDING VIDEO. H.

Hubert had attached a JPEG image file. I opened it.

"Vince," I said. He stuck his head through the hole in the wall, held up a finger, and finished up his call.

"What is it?" the detective said.

I showed him the picture Hubert had sent me. And, more important, the date that it was taken. And that's when everything changed.

CHAPTER 43

Hubert sat back and listened to the sounds outside his window. Then he entered a new command into his computer and waited. He'd been pulling at this string for a while. It kept his mind off the bruises on his face.

A batch of search results popped up on the screen. Hubert clicked on one and began to read. After a few minutes he pulled out Jim Doherty's files and pored through the old clippings a second, then a third time. Hubert shook his head. He glanced toward the kitchen knife lying flat on his desk and grinned. Like he could ever stick that into anyone.

Hubert opened up the text message and photo he'd sent out earlier in the day and thought about its implications. He wanted to try Kelly's cell again, but decided to wait until he had the details worked out. Hubert punched up the camera built into his Mac and hit RECORD. He talked for twenty minutes, laying out his thoughts while they were fresh, speculating about the curious things that were popping up in Jim Doherty's old files. He had just started a new recording file when there was a sound outside in the hallway. Hubert terminated the recording, sending a copy to Kelly, and got up. He glanced at the knife a second time, but left it on the desk and walked to the door.

CHAPTER 44

Rodriguez and I agreed. This guy had been wired into us from the start and it had to stop. No cell phone contact. No e-mail. Rodriguez would coordinate with Lawson and handle Cabrini. I'd head to the South Side and whatever waited. Somewhere along the line, I hoped one of us would find Rachel. Alive.

I checked my watch. It had already been almost an hour. I cruised the neighborhood one more time. Checked Jim Doherty's house. Then Denny and Peg McNabb. Both looked empty. Locked up tight.

I parked two blocks away and stepped out of my car. Wind from the east screamed high in the bare trees, rattling storm doors and blowing paper bags across the street. I crept through a patchwork of yards. It was dark, but I'd done my homework and didn't make a sound. Ten minutes later, I slipped over a fence, into the McNabbs' backyard. It took me less than two minutes to work the lock to the basement door free. I half expected to hear Peg's TV going upstairs, but there was nothing. I pulled out the revolver Rodriguez had given me, crept up the cellar stairs, and into the kitchen.

They were both on the floor, facedown, hands tied behind

their backs. Denny had managed to wrap one of Peg's fingers in his. And that was how I found them. Each with a single gunshot wound to the back of the head.

I checked upstairs, but the rest of the place was empty. Then I sat in the kitchen with the old couple and watched light from the street play across the house next door. A shape moved behind a window. Or maybe I just wanted it to be so. Either way, I was over the fence in what felt like a heartbeat and pressed up against the side of Jim Doherty's bungalow. Taped to the back door was a picture, flickering in the night. It was the same image Hubert Russell had sent to my phone. At least we were all on the same page.

I peeled the photo off the door, turned the knob, and walked inside. The retired cop was sitting at his kitchen table, a shotgun pointed at my chest.

"You surprised?" he said.

I looked at the photo again. It was the police graduation shot for James Nelson Doherty. He was smiling, proud and happy to be commissioned a police officer in the year of our Lord 1982.

"A smart friend of mine sent me this today," I said.

"Figured it out, huh?"

"You didn't become a cop until '82. Two years after the crash."

"So I couldn't have been a uniform up on the platform when those cars derailed. That's exactly right. Drop the gun."

Doherty had a red binder with black block lettering on the table, along with a hard black case. He had a Mac on the floor by his feet and flipped it around with his boot so I could get a look. Rachel was on-screen, blindfolded and handcuffed to a chair. There was a shotgun five feet away, locked into a shooting stand and pointed at her head. I laid my gun on the ground.

"Where is she, Jim?"

"I assume you went to Cabrini. That was clever. I'll give your woman that. But let's not waste the little time we have with loose ends."

"That include your dead neighbors next door?"

"They were very old and they died together. You have no idea what a blessing that is."

"Yeah, I envy them."

"Shut up, Michael. And sit down."

I did.

"You got it figured out yet?" Doherty said. "Or you want me to fill in the blanks?"

I held up the photo. "You were on the train."

"HELP."

I turned to the sound, coming from the doorway of the crippled CTA car. James Doherty moved his face into the broken light. His skin was the color of wet cement, his eyes, blue marbles that rolled around in his skull before settling on me.

Five feet below him, the woman with the green scarf and soft smile had been thrown against the car's back door. The accordion metal had crushed the woman's legs, and her pelvis was pinned under a twist of steel. Even that would have been okay until I saw the second piece lodged just beneath the ribs. It was the broken-off end of a girder that had split the door on impact. The girder was dark green and rusted, slick with blood, and slid in and out of her side each time she took a breath, which wasn't often enough. The woman with the soft face was dying. Even to a kid, that much was more than clear.

. . .

"I DIDN'T RECOGNIZE YOU until I saw the photo," I said.

"Sometimes life takes its pound of flesh to the bone." Doherty croaked out a laugh, and I could see the fine strands of insanity tangled up in it. "But I recognized you, Kelly. Minute you walked into the district as a rook. Same mayonnaise face you had as a kid. Still looking for his daddy."

I CRAWLED TOWARD DOHERTY, *and we pulled at the hot, rusted metal. He mumbled and prayed as we worked. Then he kissed the woman's face and tried to keep her awake. After about a minute or so, she still hadn't moved. I heard a sound from the back of the car. A CTA conductor's hat floated above us. Below it, my father's red eyes.*

"Please," I said.

Something like pity flicked across his face and I thought he might try to save her. Then the pegs were reset. My old man grabbed me by the neck and threw me toward the back of the car and the open connecting door. I hit an edge, slumped across the threshold, and felt the night on my face. I looked up at the L tracks looming above me, a couple of firemen's hats peeking over the side.

"Get out the fucking door," my old man bellowed and tried to follow me to safety.

Doherty reached out and grabbed for his leg. My old man put a boot in Doherty's face and slammed him into the side of the car. For a moment, there was nothing but a silent tremor that rippled through my fingers. Then the train lurched, this time badly. Quiet moans became screams. Steel groaned and rivets popped. A seam of metal split the length

*of the car. The woman with the soft face moaned once as
something pierced her anew. Doherty reached, but his fingers
were greased with blood, and she slipped away. Then she was
gone, leaving nothing behind but a cold wind, chasing Jim
Doherty's screams through a gaping hole to the blank pavement below.*

"HE KILLED HER," Doherty said.

I shook my head. "She would have died whether she fell or
not. The doctors told us that."

"You mean the doctors paid for by your city. He was a cow-
ard. He killed her. You both did."

I felt Doherty's eyes, crawling across my soul, finding the
dark crevices where guilt fed on a child's doubt, and a
woman's pain echoed. I shook my head free, but the man with
the shotgun had seen enough to smile.

I WAS DRAGGED UP *to the tracks in a fireman's sling. My
father, right behind me. I took one look down into the street,
but she was already covered with a sheet. They tried to talk
me into an ambulance, but I twisted away, ran from the elevated, then walked twenty blocks home. That night, my old
man drank a pint and a half of Ten High bourbon. He called
me into the kitchen sometime after midnight and asked me
what I saw on the train. I told him nothing. He beat me with
his fists, asking the same question with every blow. I kept
saying nothing because I didn't know what answer would be
better. But there was no right answer. And there was no beating that was going to hurt worse than knowing what my
father was. And knowing that every time he looked at me,*

he'd see his own cowardice reflected there. And hate me for it.

"IF I'D FOUND HIM, I'd have killed him." Doherty tilted forward in his chair, tipping the twin barrels of the shotgun a touch closer. "And maybe that would have been enough. Maybe helped both of us."

"Who was she, Jim?"

"Her name was Claire."

"Your wife?"

"Engaged."

I shifted in my chair, edging closer to my gun on the floor. "My dad's dead. I did what I could that night. You know that. So did the cops. So did the doctors."

The shotgun wavered and I could see pools of blood in his eyes, the firemen's tight features as they lifted her body off the street. Then the hard anger returned, grinding everything else to dust, wiping Jim Doherty's mind to black.

"Too late for that, Michael." He tightened his grip on the gun and let his eye wander to the image on his laptop. "I'm gonna have mine and that's just the way it is."

In his left hand, Doherty clutched a small box. He held it up for me to see. "Looks like a TV remote, doesn't it?" He nodded again toward the laptop. "It's wired to that shotgun you see there. I push the button, and the judge gets her skull air-conditioned."

"I can't bring Claire back. Nobody can."

My gun was a foot or so to my right. I inched it closer with my boot.

"Don't." Doherty pushed back from the table and kicked my piece across the room. I could feel the shotgun lift my chin, watched his finger tremble on the edge of the remote. Then he moved back to his seat. I needed to play for time.

"Tell me about Robles," I said.

"What about him?"

"Why shoot him?"

Doherty relaxed a fraction, seemed to relish the question. "I studied the classics. Not like you, but we all took a little bit back in the day."

"The *Iliad*?"

He nodded. "I told Robles about the choice Achilles once faced. Live a long, ordinary life, or die young and famous."

"Let me guess," I said. "Lake Shore Drive was Robles' day in the sun."

"Achilles chose glory and an early grave. Robles did the same. It was his fate and he embraced it."

"Guys like you love to talk about fate and destiny. Especially when your own neck's not on the line."

"You don't think I'll pay the price?"

"I don't. Do us all a favor and prove me wrong."

Doherty lifted the heavy gun again. "Not yet. Not until it's finished."

"Does that include the church?"

"It's more than that, Michael. Far more." Doherty's voice softened, stirring again the dark memories that bound us together. His eyes traveled from the image of Rachel to the red binder that sat on the table between us. "But you're right to think about the priests. Because that's where it all started."

The first bullet pinned the ex-cop's final words in his throat. He blinked once and tried to swallow. Three more rounds punched across his chest. Then Doherty fell back over his chair. Dead.

CHAPTER 45

Katherine Lawson climbed out of the darkness of the basement and nudged Doherty with the toe of her shoe. "Cocksucker."

Satisfied he was dead, Lawson lowered the gun to her side. "You all right?"

I was staring at the killer's laptop and the remote that had fallen from his fingers. The feed from wherever he kept Rachel had been cut. The image, gone.

"I'm fine," I said.

"Rachel's safe," Lawson said, stopping me with her hand as I reached for my cell. "Rodriguez told me to tell you Chubby came through."

I pointed to the laptop. "What about the video?"

"He said he'd explain it all later." She sat down at the table. "Now, why don't you give me your end of this before we call in?"

I TOLD HER about the flash drive. Then I showed her the picture of James Doherty, circa 1982.

"There wasn't a lot of time," I said. "Doherty was expecting me to head to the South Side alone. I figured you guys could still look for Rachel while I kept this guy busy."

"Bullshit. You didn't trust the feds to handle it. But you had Rodriguez bring me in to cover your ass."

"It wasn't a matter of trust."

"Not only a matter of trust, Kelly. You wanted this part to yourself." She gestured to Doherty's body.

"You think I wanted to kill him?" I said.

"Once you had Rachel secure, absolutely."

"Just like I shot the first one at the lake."

"If you weren't going to shoot him, why all the secrecy? And if you were going that route, you didn't want anyone around to come back at you on it."

I nodded to the pistol she still held loosely in a gloved hand. "Looks like you took care of that."

Lawson shook her head. "No sir. You shot Mr. Doherty." She knelt down and pressed the gun's grip into the dead man's right hand. Then she held it out to me. "You wrestled the gun away from him and shot him in the struggle. That's the only way it can go down. You're the hero. I came along afterward to applaud."

"How did you get here?"

"Drove down on my own after Rodriguez filled me in. Figured you could use a little 'unofficial' backup."

"Seems like you didn't trust me very much, either?"

"I don't like being cut out."

"And now you want me to take the weight for this?"

"How it's gotta be."

I stood up. Katherine held out an arm.

"We okay with the story?"

"You want me to be the shooter, fine. Let's go."

"**WHERE IS SHE?**" I was sitting in an FBI car, talking to Rodriguez on the phone.

"They took her to Northwestern. He had her stashed in a storage unit on Division. One of Chubby's buddies tipped us. He remembered seeing Rachel and recognized Doherty's picture."

"How bad is it?" My tongue felt thick in my mouth, all the words ill-fitting.

"She's in rough shape, Michael. Physically and mentally."

I thought about that for a moment, then forced it to the back of my mind.

"Did he have anyone watching her?"

"She was heavily sedated, and he had a couple of shotguns rigged to the door. Otherwise, I think he just depended on no one being able to trace her."

"How did you manage the video feed he had set up?"

"We did some quick surveillance before the team went in, saw the layout, and came up with a plan. The team shot their own footage of Rachel. About a minute's worth. Then we looped it and hacked into the feed Doherty was receiving before they grabbed her. That's what you were looking at. It was a risk, but the bad guy had his hands full with you and never noticed."

Doherty's face floated before me, one hand holding a shotgun, the other gripping his red binder. "He wanted me to watch someone I loved die. Just like he did."

"Fuck him, Kelly. He's dead and Rachel's not. That's what counts."

"How about the church?"

"We think we got a handle on the thing at Holy Name. I'll fill you in when you get back."

I looked through the front windshield. Federal agents had arrived in full force and were starting to process the scene. Katherine was standing in a spill of light, talking to a couple of forensic types. Under her arm, she carried Doherty's binder.

"Listen, Rodriguez, I need to talk to Hubert."

There was a pause down the line. "Actually, I'm not sure where he is," the detective said. "Feds were supposed to pick him up."

Lawson began to walk away from me, toward an evidence van. I cracked open the car door just as she ducked inside.

"Let me call you back, Vince."

I punched in Hubert's number, but got his voice mail. I called a second time and began to walk to the van. Still no answer. I found Lawson in the backseat, tagging items from inside the house.

"Hubert Russell?" I said, my heart suddenly popping in the hollow of my throat.

Lawson widened her eyes and tapped her pen against a clipboard. "What about him?"

"Where is he?"

CHAPTER 46

They had already cut Hubert down by the time we got there. I stood on the sidewalk and watched as they carried him out of his building in a coroner's bag. His memory played across the inside of my skull. I reached out, wanting to feel the weight. But he walked away from my touch and took his spot in the gallery of dead faces, waiting, apparently, to witness my grief.

"I'm sorry, Michael." Lawson stood at my shoulder, her words tight in my ear. "I don't know what happened to the team I sent in."

"It wasn't you." I stepped back from the ambulance and took a seat on the curb. "I was the one who waited. I was the one who decided he wasn't a target. And I was wrong."

"I'm sorry." Lawson crouched down and seemed to lose her train of thought, if not her composure, for a moment. "We were too late and I'm sorry."

I felt her hand on mine, her face shining white in the night.

"Michael Kelly."

I looked up. A middle-aged black woman was standing over me, removing a pair of latex gloves. Marge Connelly spent her life in the company of death, her features full of the hard grace necessary to the job. I had known her for more than a decade and seen the look before. This time I was on the receiving end.

"Hi, Marge." I stood up, Lawson with me. "This is Katherine Lawson, from the Bureau. Marge Connelly, Cook County ME."

The two women shook hands.

"You two involved in this?" Marge said.

"Hubert was a friend of mine," I said.

Marge raised her eyes a fraction and looked to the FBI agent, waiting for more.

"We might have an interest in the case," Lawson said.

"This wasn't a suicide," I said.

"Who claimed it was?" Marge opened the back door to the ambulance. The black body bag rested inside.

"What did you find?" Lawson said.

"Off the record? Death by asphyxiation. He was hung by a length of rope from his ceiling fan. How he got there?" Marge shrugged. "Just don't know right now. Young man, though. And that's an awful shame."

I moved closer to the bag. Marge slid down the zipper without a word. I took a last look, but my friend was gone, his features already cast by death's heavy hand.

"I should have something tomorrow," Marge said and closed up the bag. Lawson nodded and thanked her. Marge climbed into the front of the ambulance. Then Lawson and I watched as they took Hubert Russell to the morgue.

THE BLUE LINE

CHAPTER 47

Katherine Lawson sank into her seat and watched the wooden ties of the tracks flash beneath the window. The Blue Line train picked up speed as it left the station and leaned into a curve. Lawson laid her head against the glass, allowing the car's motion to carry her back. The first image she saw was Hubert Russell, neck stretched, spinning slowly over his desk. Then came Kelly, eyes like open coffins, holding her hand as the lid slammed shut on his friend and dirt thumped all around.

Lawson started and opened her eyes. Her train was pulling into the station at UIC–Halsted. It was just midafternoon, and the car was thankfully empty, save for a woman with tired eyes who was heading to work in her Target uniform. Lawson slipped off her black gloves and flexed her fingers. Then she laid the gloves in her lap and folded her hands over them. They were diving under the city now, into the subway, barreling toward the Loop. She looked out the window, at the banks of lights clipping past as they raced along the tunnel. The papers Lawson had copied were in her bag. She pulled them out and read through the material once again. Then she felt the key in her pocket. It opened the CTA access door near Clinton, the spot where they had found Maria Jackson's body a week ago. Lawson checked her watch. Her meeting was set for five. Plenty of time. She stood up, put on her gloves and pulled them tight. The woman in the Target uniform smiled as the train glided to a halt. Lawson smiled back. Then the doors slid open, and she stepped onto the dim platform.

LAWSON SCRAPED HER SHOES through the dirt, looking up at layers of dust floating above her in various levels of light. Jackson's body had been discovered less than a mile from where she was walking, but that wasn't the federal agent's concern. Her eyes followed a string of lights, running along the subway tracks and into the darkness. This wasn't the sealed fluorescent lighting she'd seen on her ride into the city. These were lightbulbs, old-school, just as she remembered from the Jackson crime scene. And that bothered her.

Somewhere, a rumble volleyed and echoed. Lawson instinctively stepped back and touched the grip on her gun. She could feel the vibration through her feet, hear it in the steel. The rumble grew until the train seemed like it was right on top of her. Then she saw it through a gap, a leap of fury and light, three tracks over, blowing around the corner and down the tunnel. Lawson cast her eyes overhead and watched the bulbs sway, throwing shadows on the walls around her. Then the train was past. The bulbs continued to rock in a subtle, declining arc, and soon the only sound was again the shuffle of her feet.

Lawson walked for another ten minutes, then turned back toward the door she'd come in. She'd spend the rest of her day thinking about the subway, the lightbulbs, and her meeting, all of which was good—mostly, because it kept her from thinking about the rest.

CHAPTER 48

I remembered the smell of burned wax and perfume, a door opening and cool air sucking me down a dark hallway. I stepped into a narrow room with a single overhead light and a plain wooden table. The suit motioned me to sit. He passed some paper across the table. I signed. He read what I signed and nodded. Then he left the room and returned with a vessel made of plain black stone and sealed with white wax. I pulled the vessel toward me. It felt cold and heavy in my hands. I could smell the crush of dead leaves and saw a pair of thin, bloodless lips, set in a cruel line and stitched together with dead man's silk. A shovel turned over in my mind, and the world went black. I looked up. The suit grinned and offered me the stubs of his teeth, sunken into yellow, swollen gums. I pushed the vessel back across the table and left.

Voices chased me down the hall. I could feel their eyes as I grasped the handle on the front door and nearly took it off its spindle. Then I was outside again, into the sun's blister, the blast furnace of South Central L.A., the storefront undertaker on his stoop, yelling now, telling me I needed to come back. There were more bills to pay. More credit cards to run. I *shucked my coat over my shoulder and hit it. Walked along Florence Avenue for the better part of the day, feet melting into the pavement, sun bursting inside my head. I sat on a bench at a bus stop and closed my eyes. A couple of locals hit me up for money, but I shrugged them off. Buses came, buses went. Their exhaust fused with the heat and settled into a sludge that I breathed. Finally, the sun went down and a blessed cool came into the valley of the city. I opened my eyes to headlights from the traffic and the sun dissolving orange against a blue-black sky. I took a cab to LAX. The early flights to Chicago were booked, so I caught the red-eye. I leaned back in my seat as the plane lifted off beneath me, thinking I had left my father behind. How wrong I was.*

MY EYES SNAPPED OPEN to a ceiling fan cutting lazy strokes through the late afternoon sun. My heart thundered in my chest, and my mouth felt parched.

The phone rang. I checked caller ID, lifted the phone, and dropped it back onto its cradle. Then I went into the kitchen and found the Macallan. Or what was left of it. The phone rang again. This time I picked up.

"What the fuck are you doing?" Rodriguez said.

I looked at the water glass of scotch in front of me. "Getting drunk. How about you?"

"No one's heard from you for a day and a half."

Actually, that wasn't true. Four days ago, I watched as they put Hubert Russell in a hole I'd dug for him. I spent the next three days at Northwestern Memorial. They let me in to see Rachel once. She cried until I left.

"What do you want, Rodriguez?"

"How is she?"

"Nothing's changed."

"You gonna try and see her again?"

"They said they'd call."

"You want to get a drink?"

"I'll let you know if I run out."

Rodriguez grunted and hung up. I found an old pack of ciga-rettes and lit one up. The pup didn't like that and went back into the bedroom. From the bottom drawer of my desk I pulled out a folder tabbed L.A. and opened it. On top was a police shot of my father, cold and stiff in a one-room SRO in South Central. Underneath, more of the same.

I turned the picture facedown and picked up the phone. She answered on the first ring.

"Yes, Michael."

"Anything new?"

"From an hour ago? No, Michael, nothing's new."

The woman's name was Hazel Wisdom. She worked the day shift on Rachel's floor. My contact at night was a nurse named Marilyn Bunck.

"Did she eat lunch?" I said.

"I don't know, Michael, but I'm betting yes."

"Did the doctors see her?"

"I told you. They see her every day."

"Did she talk to them?"

"I wasn't there when they examined her, but I know she's getting stronger. It's just going to take a while."

"Meanwhile, I need to keep my distance."

"It's not distance. It's space. Just a little space so she can heal."

"Doing nothing doesn't work for me, Hazel."

"Really? I hadn't noticed."

"Don't blow things out of proportion."

"You hung around here for three days, living on coffee and Snickers bars, sleeping on the floor when you weren't staring at her door and haunting every nurse and doctor that came in and out of her room."

"Until your hospital booted me out."

"It wasn't helping her, and that's what's important. Listen, if I could make it happen for you, I would. We all would. But it's just not the way these things work. You're in the business, Michael. You know."

She was right. I'd sat with plenty of them: fathers and husbands, boyfriends and brothers—victims once removed. Most would nod and gasp for air, hands clenching and unclenching, faces moving in broken pieces, lips mouthing questions for which there was never a good enough answer. And now I was one of them, asking a nurse to play God, wishing I could turn tomorrow into yesterday, wishing I could make Rachel whole. Hazel's voice brought me back to the moment.

"The truth is you just have to sit tight. Chances are she'll be asking for you. Another day or two at most."

I nodded to an empty room. "Thanks for putting up with me, Hazel."

She laughed. "For what it's worth, if I'm ever sick or hurt, I hope you're on my side."

"Be careful what you wish for. You'll call me if—"

"If she asks? What do you think?"

"Bye, Hazel."

"Talk to you in an hour, Michael."

I hung up the phone and felt the silence, heavy around me. I took my smokes and drink into the living room, and put on some music. Bruce's harmonica chased Roy Bittan up the keyboard as "Thunder Road" unwound. I took another sip of scotch, smaller this time, sat down at my desk, and clicked on my Mac. Hubert Russell's face popped up. It was the last video he made before he was murdered. His thoughts on the case I'd asked him to investigate—the case that got him killed.

"I've already sent you the police file on your pal Jim Doherty." Hubert dropped his eyes to his notes. "It's probably nothing, but you said he worked the '80 crash as a cop. As you can see, he didn't get out of the Academy until 1982."

No, he didn't, Hubert.

"Anyway," Hubert continued, "probably nothing, but whatever. I sent his Academy picture to your phone along with the file. The other thing I'm sending is about your old train crash and the company I'd mentioned, Transco."

I leaned forward and studied the digitized image of my friend. The kid was excited, knew he'd found a couple of pieces that clicked.

"Your hunch was right, Mr. Kelly. Transco and Wabash Railway were owned by the same group, a corporation called CMT Holding."

I pulled out a pad and pen and wrote CMT HOLDING at the top and TRANSCO just below it. Then I drew a line between the two. On-screen, Hubert kept talking.

"CMT appears to have had its fingers in a whole bunch of things back in the day. Railroads, related properties, manufacturing companies. All held through various subsidiaries. All very discreet. I don't have a line yet on who actually controlled CMT, but I'm working on it. The company's registered agent was an attorney named Sol Bernstein. He's dead, but I think his son might know something. So, we'll see. By the way, I also found CMT's logo." Hubert hit a few more keys. "Just sent it to your phone. A dead ringer for the one someone left on your doorstep. Cool, right?"

Hubert paused on-screen and looked to his left. "Just heard

something outside. Maybe the good guys are here to take me into protective custody." He flashed a sly grin at the absurdity of it all. "Don't worry, Mr. Kelly. If all else fails, I've got my steak knife to protect me. Talk to you later."

And then Hubert was gone. I shut down my Mac and turned up the music. Eddie Vedder had replaced the Boss and was telling me about a kid in Texas named Jeremy. I put my feet up on my desk and watched the day's light flicker and fade against the walls. By the time I finished the scotch it was mostly dark. I left my gun at home and walked down the street to find a cab. Rachel would come back, or not. But Hubert Russell was dead. And I needed to do something about it.

CHAPTER 49

Lawson's meeting was in a Loop bar and grill called the Exchequer. She got there early. He was in a back booth, sipping at a glass of water and reading the *New York Times.*

"Danielson?"

The man from Homeland Security raised his eyes from the paper and hollowed out a smile. "Agent Lawson."

Danielson made a move to get up, but Lawson waved him back down and slid in across from him.

"Thanks for seeing me on such short notice," Danielson said.

"Not a problem. What can I do for you?"

"You can start by telling me why you were wandering around in a CTA subway tunnel this afternoon."

Lawson's needle never moved off center; her response was right out of the Bureau playbook. "I work a number of cases, Mr. Danielson. All of them major crimes. So where I go and what I do is my business. Above- and belowground."

Danielson held up a pair of manicured hands. "Easy. Same side here."

"Really?"

"Yes. One of our people happened to be in the area, doing some follow-up on the Doherty thing. They saw you go in the access door at Clinton this afternoon and snapped a picture."

Danielson threw a photo across the table. Lawson picked up the picture of herself and pretended to study it. Then she scuttled it back across the table and into Danielson's lap.

"The 'Doherty thing,' as you call it, was my case, a Bureau case."

Danielson shook his head and folded up his newspaper until it was a neat rectangle. "We don't have to do this, Agent Lawson."

"No?"

"No. I'm assuming you took a look at the binder James Doherty had with him when he died."

"I collected it at the scene. Of course I looked at it."

"And you saw the notes he made?"

Lawson shrugged, but didn't respond.

"And I'm suspecting," Danielson continued, "that was why you were down in the subway today?"

Homeland Security waited, a hint of smugness tattooed across his lips.

"I'm not sure this conversation is going anywhere, Mr. Danielson."

"Weaponized anthrax, Agent Lawson. Loaded into light-bulbs and planted in Chicago's subway system. Is that what you're concerned about? What you think Mr. Doherty might have been up to?"

"From what I know—"

"What you *know*, Agent Lawson, is nothing. We've explored the possibilities raised by Mr. Doherty and the 'Terror 2000' binder. That's our job. We've discussed them with your higher-ups. And we have no concerns about any possible threat."

"Have you taken a look at Doherty's accomplice?"

"Robles, Robert R. General discharge from the United States Army in 1998. Prior to that, stationed for two years at Fort Detrick, home to this country's major bioweapons lab. Yes, we know about Mr. Robles and we've talked to the lab. He was never authorized access to any weapons materials."

"And that's it?"

Danielson fanned his hands, palms up, on the table. "As far as you're concerned, yes."

Lawson pulled out a news clipping. It was from the *Baltimore Sun*, dated February 10, 2009. The headline read:

BIODEFENSE LAB COUNTS ITS KILLERS. INVENTORY ERROR PROMPTS FORT DETRICK TO CATALOG VIRUSES, BACTERIA, OTHER MATERIALS.

"I'm sure you've seen this, Mr. Danielson. The lab director at Detrick spins it as more of a housekeeping issue—until you get to about paragraph five. That's when he tells us the probability of a 'discrepancy' regarding the lab's bioweapons inventory is 'high.' Then we learn the lab at Detrick didn't even use computers to track its inventory until 2005. Prior to that, it was all pen and paper."

"What's your point, Agent Lawson?"

"My point is this. If a guy like Robles did take a chemical agent such as mustard gas, or, here's an idea, a couple of lightbulbs filled with anthrax, would the lab at Detrick even know it?"

"Detrick has assured us their inventory is secure."

"You sound a little scared."

"Concerned, but not for the reasons you suspect. If this sort of rumor gets into the public's bloodstream, the potential fallout's enormous. For us. The Defense Department. Hell, you ever think about the city of Chicago? This place becomes a ghost town if tourists start believing there's a cloud of anthrax floating down State Street."

Danielson took another sip of his water. "As it stands, we've been able to keep the lid on the contamination at Holy Name. Barely. The last thing we need is a loose cannon of an FBI agent stirring up unrest among the locals with her doomsday scenarios."

"So you're telling me to drop this?"

"I'm telling you the water's far deeper than you suspect."

"Are you threatening me, Mr. Danielson?"

"Am I?" This time it was Danielson who showed a little bit of his teeth and Lawson who felt herself fidget. "The fact is, you're neither qualified nor authorized to even have this conversation. So clear the fuck out. If you want to take that as a threat, feel free to do so. In fact, I think you'd be wise to consider it exactly as such. Now, there's one more thing I need from you, Agent Lawson."

"What's that?"

"Everything you have on a PI named Michael Kelly."

CHAPTER 50

The Ham Tree Inn is located on a working-class stretch of Milwaukee Avenue in Chicago's Jefferson Park. I walked in around 8:00 p.m. and found a seat. The bartender wandered over. I ordered a Bud and a shot of Jim Beam. A couple of construction types had a harvest of empties in front of them and were swearing at a TV that was actually televising the Hawks game. There was another guy at the other end of the bar. Like me, he was drinking alone. I finished my whiskey and walked my can of beer over to a corner where three more guys were shooting darts. The oldest was mid-thirties, maybe six-three, two-fifty. He fit the description I'd gotten from Rodriguez. Better yet, his green Camaro was parked in the lot outside. I took a closer look. There were flecks of white paint on his face and jeans. His chest and forearms were layered with muscle, the product of working for a living. I took a sip of Bud. The older guy stepped to the line and tossed a flight of three twenties.

"Nice darts, LJ," one of his buddies said.

Larry Jennings grinned and pulled his flight from the cork. I wandered back to the bar. The three of them kept throwing. I'd just finished my second beer when Jennings popped a triple ten to win the match. He stepped in to pull his darts again. I beat him to it.

"You want these, Larry?"

He looked at me funny. "I do, pal. Thanks." He tried to grab the flight, but I pulled them back.

"Something I want you to take a look at," I said.

The place was suddenly still. Even the Hawks game seemed to go quiet. I took a white card from my pocket and stuck it on the dart board.

"This here is the mass card from Hubert Russell's funeral. You recognize the face?"

I pointed to Hubert's picture on the card. Jennings shook his head. He was confused, on his way to angry. Jennings' buddies watched from a close distance.

"Didn't think so," I said. "You beat up the wrong guy, Larry. Maybe it's time to pay."

I went back to the bar and threw down some money. There was a men's room at the end of a tight hallway, but I kept going, to the back door and an alley. I knew Jennings would follow. Guys like him always followed. Mostly because they were too afraid not to.

"YOU GOT A PROBLEM, ASSHOLE?"

He'd brought a pool cue and two of his buddies with him. The latter stayed near the doorway, drinking beer and looking like they'd rather be inside shooting darts. The former was a problem.

Jennings cut the ground between us in half with a step and swung the thick end of the cue at my head. I turned to take the blow on my shoulder. It hurt, but the cue broke in half. And I was inside.

I fired two straight lefts to the face. They were quick and short. The big man dropped to a knee and got up slowly.

"Motherfucker."

I grinned and beckoned him in. "Come and get it, sweetie."

Jennings bull-rushed. I half circled and snapped another left to the chin. Then two hard rights to the body. No emotion. Just speed, angles, and leverage.

Jennings covered up low, and I hammered a left, over his arm, into the side of his head. Then I grabbed a handful of hair and slammed his face into the side of a Dumpster. His nose pumped red. I spun him around and straightened out. Two more lefts got him going down. A short right finished it.

I'd stashed the baseball bat behind the Dumpster. I took it out and looked at the assembled crowd that now consisted of three friends. All cowards. Then I swung, two, three times. Heavy, silent blows to the body. Jennings vomited his dinner and a little blood in the alley. Part of me wanted to go for the skull. Lay the motherfucker open and let his pals pick up what was left. But murder was not on my agenda. So I dropped the bat and kicked him. Just once.

"That was for Hubert."

He lay facedown, holding his insides and moaning. I could hear noises from the street, the whisper of a car passing by, and careless laughter from a Chicago night. I choked back the darkness and moved toward the light of Milwaukee Avenue. The voice came from behind.

"Shouldn't have done that last bit. With the bat."

I turned. Jennings' buddies had been joined by the bartender, who sported an Irish brogue I hadn't caught before and held a sawed-off shotgun loosely in his hands.

"Back up against the wall, mister." The bartender tightened his grip, and I noticed a shake in the gun.

"I'm calling the cops," one of the friends said. He was squatting down by a mostly unconscious Jennings, mostly just looking at him. "He's gonna need an ambulance."

The barkeep shook his head and slid his eyes toward the back door that led to the bar. "Nobody's calling anyone. Sully, you take the boys inside. I'll be taking care of this prick myself."

I shot my hand out, pushing the short barrel up and twisting it out of the barkeep's grip. It was done without thought, without hesitation. The only way something like that can be done. Then I was holding the gun, and the Irishman was fucked. I snapped open the breech and ejected two shells.

"Came out here to do some business, did you, Irish?"

The bartender kept his mouth shut. I broke his gun into pieces against the wall.

"Your pal was right," I said. "You need to get LJ here an ambulance. If he ever wants another shot at the title, tell him to give me a call."

I took out my card and stuffed it into the Irishman's shirt pocket. Then I walked out of the alley and down the street. From inside the Ham Tree, I heard a yell for booze. The Hawks had scored and someone wanted a round.

CHAPTER 51

I woke up the next morning desperately in need of a cup of coffee and a favor. Intelligentsia provided the first. Katherine Lawson, the second.

"Where are we going?" she said and started up her car.

"I need your badge, Katherine."

She took a sip of her coffee. "Good coffee. What for?"

"I need to get inside a file down at the ME's office."

Lawson sighed. "Let me guess, Hubert Russell?"

I nodded. Lawson took a closer look at my face. "Were you in a fight last night?"

I smiled lightly. "Yeah, with a bottle of scotch."

Maybe she felt like she owed me after I took the weight on Doherty. Maybe she felt sorry for me over Rachel. Maybe she just felt sorry for me. Whatever the reason, Lawson started to drive.

"Chicago PD's taken over Hubert's case, Michael. And from what I understand, they've already closed it."

"I'm not buying it."

"Why not?"

"Timing doesn't work."

"It's close, but Doherty had enough time to kill Hubert and get back to his house."

I didn't believe it. I didn't think Lawson did either. She just needed a reason.

"Think about it, Katherine. Doherty's whole idea with Rachel's video was to lure me to the South Side so he could play his sick games."

"Which he eventually accomplished."

"Yes, and he accomplished it by giving me a false choice."

"What does that mean?"

"Doherty's plan only worked if I called Hubert and found him alive. Then when I called Doherty and got no answer, I'd head south. If I picked up on the clues Rachel left for me on the tape and went to Cabrini, the picture of the McNabbs would push me south again. The whole thing was a sucker play. A false choice with only one result. And that result required that Hubert be alive."

Lawson hit her turn signal and accelerated onto the Kennedy. "And yet he still wound up dead. How does that work? More coincidence?"

She was right. I hadn't figured that part out. Lawson pressed her advantage.

"Who else could it have been, Michael? Who else wanted Hubert Russell dead?"

"I don't know."

"That's right. You don't. Because there is no one else. No one but Doherty. He hated you for whatever fucked-up reason he had, and maybe he killed your friend to even the score. You know damn well he would've killed Rachel if he'd gotten the chance."

"A chance you didn't give him, right?"

"I'm not looking for that, Michael."

"I guess I should thank you."

"Look, we'll go down to the ME. You ask your questions. But if nothing turns up, you let it go." Lawson looked over. "All right?"

"Yeah."

We drove in silence for a while. Lawson put on an Alicia Keys CD.

"How is Rachel?" she said.

"Not good."

Lawson peeked over again. "You want to talk about it?"

"No."

"All right." She kept driving. I pulled out my notes.

"Can I ask you something else?" I said.

"Sure."

"The binder we found down in Doherty's house."

"Which binder?"

"You know which binder. The red one. Doherty had it with him. Looked like he was going to show me something—"

"Right before I shot him."

"That's right. And then you grabbed the binder before I could get a look at it."

Lawson was shaking her head. A hint of something played reluctantly across her lips. She reached over and turned up her music. I turned it down.

"You don't want to talk about the binder?" I said.

"Why do you need to know?"

"What is there to know?"

"Exactly, Michael. What is there to know? As far as you're concerned, nothing."

"Now you got me curious."

"Bullshit. You were curious from the moment you saw it. And I think you might have gotten at least half a look at it."

"You're not gonna tell me about the binder?"

She turned the music up again. I returned to my notes.

"What's that?" She pointed to a file I had tabbed TRANSCO.

"A lead Hubert was working on the old CTA crash," I said. "Most of it's in the files he downloaded to you."

"That for the ME?"

"Maybe. You want to hear?"

"Hang on." Lawson had exited the highway. Now she took a right onto Harrison Street and pulled into a slot in front of the Cook County Medical Examiner's building. I handed her the folder.

"I'm listening," she said and began to leaf through Hubert's notes.

I explained how a faulty device built by Transco derailed a train thirty years ago and probably killed eleven people.

"Who owned Transco?" she said, eyes narrowed, still glued to her reading.

"An old holding company named CMT." I handed her some more paperwork. "Hubert could never nail down the principals, but I think it's worth a little more digging."

Lawson closed the folder and handed it back to me. "Why?"

"Because I get the feeling these guys, whoever they are, don't want to be discovered."

"And that interests you?"

"I don't believe Doherty killed Hubert." I popped open the passenger's-side door. "And these guys have something to hide. So, yeah, that interests me. Let's go."

CHAPTER 52

What makes you think I wouldn't have given you a look?"

Marge Connelly measured me through a pair of black reading glasses and reached for her coffee mug. She was sitting behind her desk, dressed in a set of blue scrubs, with a stack of files in front of her.

"Why would you?" I said.

Connelly puffed out her cheeks and pulled the rest of her face into a frown. "Agent Lawson, I don't know you very well, but I'm going to ask you a question."

"Nothing you say leaves this room," Lawson said. "You have my word."

The ME sighed and pulled a folder from the pile on her desk. "What concerns me is the way the case is being handled." She flipped the file open. "If you know what I mean?"

"I think I know what you mean," I said, "but fill me in."

"First day or so, there's the kind of interest you'd expect. Mayor's office calling, higher-ups in Homicide, even the feds." Connelly glanced toward Lawson, who crossed her legs and kept her hands folded in her lap.

"So we push up the autopsy, blood work, all that stuff," Connelly continued. "I get the results, call everyone, nothing."

"What do you mean 'nothing'?" I said.

"Just that. The mayor's office gave it a yawn. Feds never even called me back." Another look Lawson's way. "Homicide told me to send the results along when I got a chance. So I packaged it all up and sent it off."

"Our office did inquire," Lawson said, "but backed off once we saw the lay of the land."

Marge Connelly leaned forward in her chair. "Which is what exactly, Agent Lawson?"

"Chicago PD has taken over primary investigation of the case," Lawson said. "And I believe they've concluded James Doherty was responsible for Hubert's death."

Connelly frowned. "Explain."

"It's not something that's been in the press," Lawson said, "but Hubert was working the Doherty case."

The ME picked up Hubert's file. "*This* boy was working *that* case? How did that happen?"

"He was helping me, Marge," I said.

"You were working that case?" Connelly shook her head, but let it go. "What is it, exactly, you're looking for?"

"I don't know," I said. "What did you find?"

Connelly plucked a summary page from the folder. "Ligature mark on the neck consistent with hanging. The rope was nothing special. Something you could buy in a hardware store. Slipknot. More common in a suicide, but it still works for murder." Connelly glanced up and over her glasses. "Then there are the wrists."

"What about them?" I said.

"My examination revealed marks on both of the decedent's

wrists. Can't be a hundred percent, but they could have been made by a set of handcuffs." Connelly laid the summary page back down on her desk.

"You have pictures of the autopsy?" I said.

The ME pulled out a stack of photos. Hubert's skin looked slightly blue under the lights. White loops of stitching held together the Y incision across his shoulders and down his chest. I passed the photos over to Lawson.

"Here's a shot of the ligature mark." Connelly moved another stack of photos across. "And these are the shots of his wrists."

The ligature mark was a single oblique line three-quarters of the way around Hubert's neck, purple to the point of black. Lawson picked up a photo of Hubert's right wrist.

"Can I take a look?" I said. Lawson snapped her eyes onto mine and pushed the picture across.

"Possible cuff marks are here and here," Connelly said, pointing with her pen.

"Anything else?" I said.

Connelly shrugged. "Blood work was clean. No sign of any drugs introduced into the body."

I took a closer look at the ligature mark, then both wrists. Lawson stirred beside me.

"Michael, I've got a couple of meetings this morning."

I looked over. "You gotta run?"

She nodded. I glanced at Connelly.

"Be all right if I stick around and go through this stuff some more?"

The ME shrugged. "Okay by me. No one else seems too interested."

I turned back to Lawson. Her eyes floated across my face. Connelly got up from behind her desk.

"I've got a couple of things I need to take care of. Michael, you can look through the materials in here. Agent Lawson, a pleasure to meet you." The two women shook hands, and Marge Connelly left, closing the door behind her.

"You think this is the best thing, Michael?"

"What can it hurt?" I said, pulling Hubert Russell's autopsy folder toward me.

Katherine Lawson slipped her hand across the back of mine. "Let go of the file and look at me."

I did, head pounding, heart suddenly rolling in my chest.

"Hubert's not your fault."

I began to speak. She shook her head.

"You had every reason to think he'd be safe in his apartment. I could have, should have, followed up and made sure my agents got there quicker than they did. Truth is, there are probably a lot of people who let Hubert down. But you know what, Michael? You're not one of them."

"You think I'm wasting my time here?" I said.

"I think you're chasing a ghost."

I laughed. "That's what Jim Doherty told me when I approached him about his old files."

"This isn't going to end like that, Michael. Doherty killed Hubert. You know it. So do I. It's time to let it go. Time to heal."

Then Katherine Lawson leaned in and kissed me. Softly. Her fingertips brushed across my cheek, leaving behind a tenderness I couldn't afford.

"I gotta do this," I said.

She hesitated, as if she wanted to say more, but nodded instead. "Let me know if I can help." Then she stood up and left.

I spread Hubert's file out on the desk and began to sort

through it all over again. An hour later, I was elbow deep in autopsy photos when I saw something. Or something that might be something. I found Marge Connelly in the middle of cutting off the top of someone's skull. I waited for her to finish.

"What?"

"When you get a chance," I said.

"Is it important?"

"Could be."

Connelly stepped away from the table, snapped off her gloves, and followed me back to her office.

"WHAT IS IT, MICHAEL? By the way, the agent and you?" Marge raised a discreet eyebrow.

"No," I said and picked up one of the autopsy photos. "This photo here. Hubert's left wrist."

Connelly slipped her glasses back on and squinted. "That's a shot of the back of the wrist."

I pulled out a second photo. "This is the right wrist. Basically, the same shot."

"What about it?"

"Here." I pointed to the left wrist. "About an inch below the indentation you said might be a cuff mark. There's a second discoloration. Looks like it might be some sort of bruise."

Marge leaned in and took a closer look. Then she slipped over to her computer and booted it up.

"We have these photos on file. Let me see if I can blow that area up."

Marge found the shot and began to work on it. I watched as

she zoomed in and sharpened the image. After a couple of minutes she sat back. "That's the best I can do."

"What do you think?"

She touched the screen with a pencil. "This area right here is what you're talking about, right?"

"Yeah." It was definitely a bruise, more circular than I'd first thought. "Doesn't seem like it could have been made by the cuff."

"I agree," Marge said. "It's almost round in shape. Damn, I'm sorry I missed this."

"You didn't miss it. We got it right here. What do you think?"

"Judging by the discoloration, I'd say it was certainly made at or around the time of death. Beyond that, I don't know."

"Guess?"

Marge looked at the photo and tapped the pencil to her teeth. "Let me try a few more things before I give you an answer."

"Like what?"

"We have a tool we use on bite marks. Brings out the detail in any indentations on the victim's skin. Not always accepted in court, but pretty damn effective." Connelly leaned forward and took another look at the photo. "Let me run this through the program. See what we get."

"How long?"

Marge shrugged. "Hell, we can do it this afternoon. I'll give you a call."

"Great. And, Marge, if we find something, what happens to your report?"

The ME smiled. "My report's done, Michael. Case closed. Just like the city wants it."

CHAPTER 53

Faces and facts mixed and mingled in a kaleidoscope of color and sound. Jim Doherty, features sunken and feral, nursing his hatred in a tomb of darkness under the city. A shooter named Robles, eyes gray and flat, rifle flashing death along the lakefront. An alley off Milwaukee Avenue and a young man with a rope around his neck. Rachel, staring into the corners of her mind, watching the past cut her present into little pieces. Katherine Lawson and the trace of her hand on my face. Mayor John J. Wilson. A company called Transco and an autopsy file. A red binder.

The pieces of this case, maybe two or three cases, held together by the thinnest of wires: circumstance and an educated guess. The rest floated and turned in the darkness, offering themselves up as a piece of the puzzle, with no real clue as to how or why.

I sighed and opened my eyes. This was fucked. I got out of my car, walked down Broadway and up a flight of stairs. There was a stack of mail shoved up against the door to my office. On top was a thick manila envelope. The return address was handwritten in black felt pen:

SOL BERNSTEIN JR.

110 SUTTER STREET

SAN FRANCISCO, CALIFORNIA

Son of a bitch. I found my way to my desk, opened up the blinds, and sliced the seal on the envelope. By the turning light of late afternoon, I read Mr. Bernstein's letter.

MR. KELLY,

I HOPE THIS MISSIVE FINDS YOU WELL. AS YOU PROBABLY KNOW, YOUR ASSOCIATE HUBERT RUSSELL CONTACTED ME IN REFERENCE TO A COMPANY NAMED TRANSCO AND ITS PARENT COMPANY, CMT HOLDING. MY LATE FATHER WAS INVOLVED WITH CMT MANY YEARS AGO, ACTING AS ITS ATTORNEY IN SOME MATTERS, AS WELL AS ITS REGISTERED AGENT. FORGIVE ME FOR NOT CONTACTING MR. RUSSELL DIRECTLY, BUT, AT THE RISK OF SOUNDING PRESUMPTUOUS, HE SOUNDED A BIT YOUNG, ALBEIT QUITE CAPABLE, OVER THE PHONE. I HOPE YOU UNDERSTAND AND EXTEND MY APOLOGIES AND BEST WISHES TO YOUR COLLEAGUE.

AS TO TRANSCO AND CMT, I HAVE THOUGHT A GREAT DEAL ABOUT THE MATTER AND DECIDED YOUR INQUIRY MIGHT BE AN OPPORTUNITY TO PUT SOME THINGS TO REST. I AM INCLUDING A RAFT OF DOCUMENTS I FOUND AMONG MY FATHER'S PAPERS. I THINK THE MATERIAL IS FAIRLY SELF-EXPLANATORY. I WILL INCLUDE A NUMBER BELOW, SHOULD YOU NEED TO REACH ME, BUT I SINCERELY ASK THAT YOU DO NOT. DISCRETION IS OF THE UTMOST IMPORTANCE TO ME AS I, LIKE MY FATHER, AM AN ATTORNEY WITH A SENSITIVE AND VERY PRIVATE PRACTICE. I CONSIDERED GOING DIRECTLY TO THE AUTHORITIES WITH THIS INFORMATION,

BUT COLLEAGUES IN CHICAGO ASSURE ME YOU ARE EXPERI-
ENCED IN AFFAIRS SUCH AS THESE AND CAN BE COUNTED
ON TO ACT IN A CONFIDENTIAL AND EXPEDITIOUS MANNER.
I HOPE I HAVE MADE A WISE DECISION.

SINCERELY,

SOL BERNSTEIN JR.

I weighed the bundle in my hand and then cracked it open. On top were several Transco engineering reports from 1974 to 1979, detailing internal concerns about the company's prod- ucts, including a suggested recall of its engine overrides. I scanned the old reports and laid them aside. Underneath were a number of old contracts stapled together, share certificates, and personal correspondence. I took my time with the mate- rials, pulling out a pad and pen to take notes as I read. When I was finished, I sat back and stared at the ceiling. On a single piece of paper I had sketched out the web of companies owned by CMT Holding, including Transco, Wabash Railway, and a number of related businesses and properties stretching back ninety years. At the bottom of the page, I wrote down the name of the entity that controlled all of them—the entity responsible for the L crash on February 4, 1980.

I pulled out the black-and-yellow logo Hubert had ID'd as belonging to CMT, as well as the Old English script from Wabash Railway. I hadn't noticed before, but the CMT train carried an odd *t* shape on the very front of its engine. I took a closer look at the Wabash script. The *l* in "Railway" had a small bar across it, making it into a lowercase *t* as well. Or, in both cases, maybe a couple of crosses. Fucking hell.

Forty minutes later, I was still piecing through the old papers when my phone rang. Marge Connelly had worked her magic with the autopsy photo. I downloaded the shots and talked to the medical examiner for another hour. Then I thanked her and hung up.

I closed my eyes and visualized all those pieces of the puzzle, still floating in the darkness. Slowly, one, then another, then a third stopped turning. They hung before my mind's eye, slipped neatly together and locked into place. The picture sharpened, and a face came into focus. I printed out the photos the ME had sent me, packed up Sol Bernstein's paperwork, and locked up the office on my way out.

CHAPTER 54

I should have known when I didn't hear the pup at the front door. But my mind was somewhere else, sunk into the tangled depths of CMT Holding and a single autopsy photo. I was halfway across my living room when I looked up and saw her, wagging her tail and sitting comfortably in the lap of the mayor of our good city, the honorable John J. Wilson.

"Nice dog, Kelly. I should have kept this one." The mayor gave Maggie a scratch behind the ears and set her on the floor. Then he gestured to the two men sitting on either side of him.

"These are federal agents. They want to ask you some questions."

I took the only chair left in the room and considered the pair of suits, one black, one blue. If they weighed two hundred pounds between them, they were lucky. Behind them was the muscle, a linebacker type, wearing a gray cashmere overcoat, finished with black leather gloves and Maui Jim wraparounds.

"What about the Terminator back there?" I said.

Wilson waited for someone else to speak. When no one did,

he shrugged. "I told them you could be reasoned with, but they were wary. Of the gun and all that."

"And you just came along for the ride?"

Wilson stretched his thick lips into a thin line. "I came along to protect the city's interests, Kelly. And maybe yours, as well."

"I'm listening," I said.

Blue suit thumped a briefcase onto my coffee table and snapped it open. I caught a glimpse of red inside and got an idea where this might be headed. Then the suit opened his mouth and I got an even better idea.

"Mr. Kelly, my name is Leo Nolan. This is Dr. Matthew Danielson. We work with Homeland Security."

Nolan didn't flash an ID and I didn't ask for one.

"We know you were involved in the capture and death of James Doherty," Nolan continued. "We also know he talked to you about a red binder he had in his possession at the time he was shot."

"I never got a look inside the binder," I said. "Agent Lawson took it with her from the scene."

Nolan nodded. "And yet, we have reason to believe you continue to make inquiries about the binder and the nature of its contents."

"And how would you know that, Mr. Nolan?"

Nolan shuffled through his briefcase for some paperwork. "We operate under a federal directive called the Cyber Initiative. Allows us, among other things, to monitor computers and Internet activity that might pose a threat to national security."

I looked at the mayor, who shrugged. "That's as much as they told me, Kelly. Maybe you can explain the rest."

I turned to Nolan. "The red binder you're talking about is a Pentagon report issued in 1998, called 'Terror 2000.' Yes, I saw the title when we were in Doherty's house. And yes, I did some searching about it on the Internet."

"Why?" Nolan said.

"Why not? A guy like Doherty carries something like that around with him, it gets my attention. How about you?"

Nolan flicked a piece of lint off his pants. "Did Mr. Doherty make any specific threats?"

"That's what Mr. Doherty did best."

"Specific threats against the city?"

I glanced toward the black suit named Danielson. "Does he ever talk?"

Nolan blinked behind his tortoiseshell frames. "Answer the question, Mr. Kelly."

"No, he didn't give me any indication as to what he had planned. I think he was about to when things got out of control."

Nolan leaned in. "And you shot him?"

I nodded. "Whatever Doherty was planning, the details died with him. For what it's worth, however, I might have some ideas."

Danielson shifted in his seat and finally spoke. "We're not interested in your fucking ideas, Mr. Kelly. We're here for the black case you took from Doherty's house. Hand it over and this discussion is at an end. Persist with all the bullshit and we move to another phase."

I looked up at the Terminator and smiled. Behind him was a closet. Inside it, on the top shelf, the black case they were looking for. I returned my gaze to Danielson. "I don't know anything about any case."

Danielson rolled his eyes toward Nolan, who glanced at Wilson. The mayor touched a finger to his lips.

"Gentlemen, let me have a minute."

Danielson didn't like the idea. Nolan took him aside and talked in his ear. Danielson relented and held up five fingers. "Five minutes, Mr. Mayor."

He and Nolan picked up their coats and took a walk. The Terminator followed. I noticed he dragged his left foot and hoped it hurt like hell. Wilson waited until the door had closed before speaking. "What do you want, Kelly?"

"How do you know I want anything?"

"How many times have we talked where you didn't want something?"

"I get the feeling you know as little about these guys as I do."

"Homeland Security?"

I nodded. The mayor picked up Maggie again and stroked the top of her head. The pup's eyes immediately began to close.

"You know how many times I get called into meetings with these stiffs?" Wilson said. "First time it happened, three months after 9/11, we went into full fucking pucker. They sat around, bullshitting for a couple of hours, never gave us a sniff as to what was going on. Poison in the water? Crop dust downtown with some evil-sounding shit? Suitcase nuke in the Hancock? Who the fuck knows? And then you know what I figured out? Who the fuck cares."

"I don't believe that, Mr. Mayor."

Wilson held up a hand. "Hear me out. Of course I care. My point is, what can we do? Someone decides to blow themselves up in the Water Tower this afternoon, what's Chicago PD going to do? Nothing except clear the street so we can get the ambulances in. We don't have the expertise, we don't have the manpower, and we sure as hell don't get the heads-up from the feds in enough time to do anything even if we did have any of the other shit. So what's my point, right?"

I nodded.

"My point is one I learned a long time ago. When Homeland Security shows up, we smile and go along. Listen to their happy horseshit, express appropriate concern, and send them on their way. If they catch the bad guy, great."

"And if not?"

"That's the beauty of it. So far there hasn't been any 'if not.' At least not in this town, knock on fucking wood. But, really, that's all we can do. That and manage the threat."

"What does that mean?"

"You know what the estimated death totals would be for one of these doomsday attacks?"

I shook my head.

"Fifty, hundred thousand. If the fuckers got lucky, maybe a million or more." Wilson chuckled at the impossible piles of imaginary dead. "If it's biological, we couldn't even bury the dead. Have to burn 'em in funeral pyres. Funeral pyres, Kelly. People can't handle that shit. So we manage the message. Keep it positive. Serious and focused, but never too scary. That's the whole job."

"So the *idea* of Armageddon is actually much worse than the real thing?"

"Exactly. Now, take your asshole Doherty. He doesn't have any mass fucking weapons. He was bullshitting you the whole time."

"How about Holy Name?"

"How about it? He threatened to contaminate all of our churches, people would die, blah, blah, bullshit, blah. Then what does he do? Throws a little ammonia in the cathedral's holy water."

"It was a little more than ammonia."

"All right, all right. Glorified ammonia. Thing is, how many people died? How many are still in the hospital? Zero. He was full of shit, just like the rest of these motherfuckers. I don't tell anyone this, but they got lucky on 9/11. Incredibly lucky. And we're going to spend the rest of this century and untold billions waiting for that other shoe."

"One that's never gonna drop?"

"Not on my watch. So don't worry about Doherty. If he could have torched this city, he would have. He just wanted to fuck with people, especially you. Then he wanted to kill your girl while you watched. And thank God he didn't."

"What do you need from me?"

"Give them the case and let's move on."

"You think I have it?"

"We know you do. Lawson mentioned it in a report she filed. Said she didn't think the thing was important, but saw it in Doherty's kitchen. Saw you pick it up. These guys heard that and got all hot and bothered."

"You want to know what's inside?"

"Not really."

"There's nothing inside. Just two Styrofoam cutouts where something used to be."

"See, more nothing. Give them the case, Kelly. You may think you're John Wayne, and maybe you are. But the feds don't give a shit. They'll roll right over you and never miss a beat."

Wilson lowered his eyelids as he leaned down and kissed Maggie on the top of the head. "She's a good pup, Kelly. She likes it here."

I thought about the black case. About my conversation with Marge Connelly. About making things right. "I need something in return."

"Fucking ballbreaker." Maggie lifted her eyes as the mayor shifted in his seat.

"Something that stays between me and you," I said. "Actually, it's something you might enjoy."

Wilson dropped my pup gently to the floor and leaned forward, long nostrils quivering, hoping to catch a scent. "Fucking ballbreaker. What do you got?"

So I told him. Some of it. He licked his lips and grinned.

"The evil fucking empire. Gotta tell you, Kelly, I'm a little impressed."

The black case was forgotten, at least for the moment, as I laid out the rest of my proposal to the mayor. All in all, I was pretty sure it made his day.

CHAPTER 55

The wind kicked a heavy boot against my windows. It was coming up on 7:00 a.m., and I hadn't been to bed. I sipped some coffee and looked outside. A sparrow stared back, black eyes flicking over mine, feathers ruffling against the elements. I moved my eyes down to the folder on my desk. Inside it was everything I'd need for the day's business. On top of the file was my gun. I slipped the gun into its holster and looked through the file one more time.

I'd given Homeland Security its black case and whatever tale it told. Then I went to work, scraping together what I needed from the files I had, the Internet, and a few phone calls. The mayor had called around eleven, and again at midnight. He'd given me the bits and pieces I'd asked for. Hadn't asked too many questions. Hadn't had anyone else sit in on our conversations. The mayor was too smart for that.

I flipped the folder shut and looked back out the window. The sparrow was still there, still clinging to its perch. I took another sip of coffee. The bird lifted its wings and was gone, leaving nothing behind but a bare branch, shivering in the wind.

My phone rang. Rodriguez's cell number flashed up on caller ID. It was the third time he'd called that morning. I ignored it and walked into my bedroom, Maggie close on my heels. Her crate was sitting beside the bed, along with a bag of food and her toys. I sat down, the pup in my lap. She immediately rolled over for a belly rub. I obliged.

"You be a good girl," I said and picked her up. She licked my face. I held her for a moment. Then I put her into her crate and slid the latch over.

I loaded the pup, her food, and the toys into my car and headed south on Lake Shore Drive. The hospital had called, asking for anything from home that might make Rachel feel more secure, more relaxed. It was a short list, one that didn't include me.

I pulled up to Northwestern Memorial. Hazel Wisdom was waiting in the lobby.

"I could use a smoke," she said. I nodded and we stepped outside.

"It's just for a couple of days, Michael."

"It's okay," I said.

Maggie scratched at the bars. She didn't like the crate. I couldn't blame her.

"She's a cute dog," Hazel said.

"Yeah, she's pretty easy. Just feed her when she's hungry, walk her when she has to go, and let her do whatever she wants the rest of the time, and you should have no problems."

"Sounds like a few doctors I know."

"I bet."

"Rachel's getting better, Michael."

"Like you said, there's nothing I can do but wait." I finished my cigarette and flipped the butt into the wind. "So that's what I'm gonna do."

Hazel gave me a hug and I handed the crate over. The pup stared at me as she disappeared into the hospital. I wanted to wave, but felt like an idiot. Instead, I got back in my car, the file folder on the front seat beside me.

CHAPTER 56

An hour later, I pulled into an industrial park in the 700 block of South Jefferson. The sky was heavy with the promise of rain. The lot, empty. I tugged a black knit hat low over my eyes and walked three blocks with my head down. The cops had taken down the tape from Maria Jackson's murder, but I took a quick look around anyway.

The CTA access door was unlocked this time. A single bulb did yeoman's work, painting a swath of white against rough walls and the run of stairs. I spiraled down until I hit bottom. Then I stepped out, for the second time, into Chicago's subway system.

The light down here was brighter, it seemed, than the night I'd found Jackson's body. I walked in the opposite direction, across a switchback and alongside an old spur of track. A half mile in, I came to a curve. To my left was a small door, with the word MAINTENANCE stenciled in black on a beige wall. That's where I found her, sitting on a beat-up bench.

"Michael, you found it."

"Sorry, I'm late. I got tied up."

I moved a little closer. Katherine Lawson was wearing a

black leather coat and kept her hands in her pockets. Behind her was a row of old lockers, most with their doors missing.

"What do you think of the place?" She withdrew a gloved hand and swung it around the tiny room. "Maria Jackson's body was found about a hundred yards down the tracks from where you came in. They found this little shed while they were working the scene."

"That's nice, Katherine. Why did you want to meet me here?"

I had wanted to set up my own meeting with the FBI agent and struggled with time and place. Then she'd called late last night and did the heavy lifting for me.

"You mean why not a drink like normal people?" Her laugh sounded flat and never reached her eyes. "There's a few things we need to talk about, Michael. A few things we need to take a look at."

Lawson pulled a sheaf of papers from her pocket. "You asked about Jim Doherty's red binder the other day. I copied some pages for you. Thought you might want to take a look."

I shook my head. "Had a long talk with the mayor. He convinced me the binder really wasn't worth my time."

"I'm sorry about that," she said. "I didn't realize Homeland Security would get involved. Otherwise, I never would have filed that report."

"You heard about their visit?"

"I got one, too. There's something about the Doherty thing that bothers me, Michael. Something I think we're missing."

"I know what you mean."

She held up her fistful of paper. "It has to do with the binder and the tracks near where Jackson's body was found. Let me show you, then you can take a pass if you want."

I sat down opposite her on the bench. "There's something else we should talk about first."

"What's that?" she said.

I took out my folder and placed it on top of the paperwork she had already spread out between us. She looked, but didn't touch.

"Does this have to do with Doherty?" she said.

"Open it up and take a look."

She flicked the edge of the file open. I kept talking.

"The top set of papers comes from 1978. Outlines the ownership structure for Transco and its holding company, CMT."

Her eyes shimmered in the jaundiced light. "The company you think caused the old train accident?"

"Yeah."

Lawson flipped through the documents and twisted her face into a smile. "Is this supposed to mean something to me?"

"I'm guessing you came across it when you worked the case on Father Mark. He was ripping off his parish, and someone made the mistake of giving you a look at the archdiocese's books."

"Everyone knows I worked that case, Michael."

"What they didn't know about was CMT Holding."

Lawson didn't say anything, but I could see the muscle in her jaw pumping like a piston.

"You know how much money the Chicago archdiocese takes in every year, Katherine? A little more than a billion dollars. Cash money. Tax-free. Not even an IRS form to file. Nice work if you can get it."

I waited, but Lawson just sat there, hands in her pockets, and listened.

"CMT was set up in the 1920s. It's a tangled trail, but a lawyer named Bernstein provided me with a map. The seed money came from the archdiocese's coffers. A greedy cardinal's way to secretly invest in a little property, a few railroads. Make a little coin he didn't have to share with the parishioners. CMT got bigger over time. Cardinals and bishops got greedier with each passing generation. Created a web of related businesses, subsidiaries like Transco. Then 1980 happened. The crash at Lake and Wabash and eleven people dead. Blood the men in collars needed to get clean of. So they divested themselves of everything, dissolved CMT, and walked—no, ran—away and hid. Then you came along."

Finally, something had caught her interest, and Lawson stirred. "Excuse me?"

Among other things, the Honorable John J. Wilson keeps a man named Walter Sopak on his personal payroll. Sopak is what's known as a forensic accountant—a guy who knows how to hide your money and how to find out where someone else's is hidden. I've never met the man. Wilson made sure of that. But I pulled Sopak's report on Katherine Lawson from the folder.

"You make a little over a hundred thousand a year, Katherine. Your parents are dead. They left you a nice set of teeth and a pile of debt. Still . . ." I tapped Sopak's report. "There's the condo in Sante Fe and a timeshare in Italy. Hidden pretty well, but there they are. And then there's the money that goes offshore and just disappears. Even the guy who put this report together wasn't sure he found it all, but he made a pretty good guess."

"Guess at what, Michael?"

"He figures you're good for maybe one to two million a year, minimum, from whoever keeps the church's secrets. Maybe seven to ten million total over the last five years."

"You're crazy," she said.

"Am I?"

"Either that or you need a long vacation."

I pulled out the unregistered .38 Rodriguez had given me to use on Doherty. "You got a gun, Katherine?"

She ran her eyes to the tracks behind me and back. "I have my service weapon, Michael." She showed me the Glock on her hip.

"Stand up, take it out, and put it on the ground."

She did.

"Now, what else do you have?"

"What the hell does that mean?"

"You want me to cuff you and run your pockets?"

She pulled a black-handled revolver out of her coat pocket and laid it on the ground beside the first.

"Why the second piece, Katherine? I'm thinking you might be worried about our talk the other day? Maybe take me for a walk down the tracks?"

"You've been under a lot of stress, Michael. Just put the gun down and we'll figure it out."

I pulled an envelope from my pocket. Inside it was a stack of photos. Ordered and marked. I laid them faceup on the bench.

"You know what that top picture is?"

She shook her head.

"It's a shot taken from one of the mayor's traffic cameras. Wilson likes to ticket people 24/7. Anyway, this one is set up a half block from Hubert Russell's building. Shot was taken the day he died. You see the black SUV there?"

She took a look at the shot, but didn't seem all that interested.

"That's your car, Katherine."

"Of course it is. I was back and forth processing that scene."

"Take a look at the time stamp. Four-twenty p.m., twenty minutes after Rodriguez talked to you on the phone and almost a half hour before the first agents got there. Agents you sent."

"This is bullshit, Michael. Put the fucking gun down."

"Flip over the next picture, Katherine."

"No."

"Flip it over," I said and felt the mist begin to rise behind my eyes. Maybe she felt it, too, because she turned up the next picture. It was one of Marge Connelly's autopsy photos.

"This is a shot of Hubert's wrist. Actually, it's the back of his left wrist. Remember the ME told us she found some marks that might have come from a set of cuffs? I took a closer look after you left and found something else."

I pointed with one hand, kept the gun steady in the other. "You see the round mark there? It's actually a bruise. Made at roughly the time of death. Flip over the next photo."

This time she did it without complaint.

"This is a blowup of the same shot," I said. "Now you can see the indentations in the skin. The ME thinks they were made by a ring. She figures someone was wrestling with Hubert, maybe trying to bind his wrists or slip on a set of cuffs."

I flipped over the last photo myself.

"The state has this computer program that can enhance these things even further." I pointed with the tip of the barrel. "Right here you can make out the *F* and a *B* pretty clearly. We checked the script. That's 'FBI,' Katherine, made by an Academy graduation ring. And you see this half circle here and the straight line beside it? Expert tells me that's a *K* and the beginning of an *M*. Initials, 'KML,' maybe? Katherine Marie Lawson?"

I looked down at her gloved hands, the FBI ring I knew she was wearing underneath.

"You want to tell it?" I said. "Or you want me to?"

Lawson raised her chin and didn't say a word.

"I don't know exactly how you found out about CMT and Transco, but you did," I said. "That was their mistake. Still, a couple of million a year was pocket change to keep you quiet, especially when laid up against criminal conspiracy and eleven charges of negligent homicide. Church doesn't need that kind of publicity. No matter how long ago it was."

"Don't underestimate the human capacity for greed, Michael."

"Fair enough. For a while, everything was sweet. You got your money and kept your mouth shut. Then James Doherty came along and started killing people. You saw the possible connection right away, but figured there was still no real danger, until I mentioned the old crash when we were at Four Farthings. That got things percolating. After that, you were keen to get a look at Hubert Russell's work, see where it was headed. When Hubert sent you his notes, you saw how good the kid was, how relentless he could be, how inevitable it was that Transco would be uncovered and the church exposed. Couldn't let that happen. Couldn't let the golden goose be killed. Could you, Katherine?"

"You're seriously unbalanced."

"So you killed Hubert instead. I don't know if anyone connected to the church was in on it. Or maybe you were just protecting an investment. Either way, you didn't plan it out the way you'd like. Didn't have time. When Rodriguez gave you Hubert's address and told you he was a possible target, you saw an opportunity. If Doherty had already killed Hubert, perfect. If not, you could take care of him and still try to pin it on

Doherty. So you hustled over to the kid's apartment yourself and found Hubert very much alive. He saw your badge and let you into the apartment without a second thought.

"Somewhere along the line you realized Doherty probably had to go as well. Before he could tell me what he knew about the church. Before he could convince me there was no way he killed my friend. You knew I was at Doherty's house, hunting him. So you headed down after you finished with Hubert. You got lucky, walked in on us, and shot Doherty where he sat."

"Is that it?" she said.

"One question. Why hang him?"

I could see the tumblers clicking behind her eyes, assessing the odds, figuring a way to play me. I could have told her not to waste her time.

"I'm guessing you only had your service weapon and couldn't use that." I shrugged. "If the Doherty angle fell through, there was always suicide. Hubert was young and vulnerable. As a fallback, it might have worked."

"You really think you can prove any of this?" she said.

"If whoever's been paying you talked, it wouldn't be a problem. But I'm thinking some people might look at the church as the bigger fish here. Decide to cut their deal with you." I raised my gun. "And I can't have that, Katherine."

I watched as reality sank in and the hard sheen cracked, then crumbled. Her features fell off her face, one by one, sucked backward into a hole punched by fear. Not of being poor. Nor of being alone. Simply of being dead. Dead and lying in the dirt and soot of Chicago's subway.

I read all of that in her face. And then she looked behind the gun. To the person holding it. And Katherine Lawson began to rally.

"You can't do it," she said, more to herself. "You couldn't

pull the trigger on Doherty. You couldn't pull the trigger on Robles. You can't do it now." And then she smiled. And that was a mistake.

I lowered the gun and shot her once in the thigh. The recoil echoed off the hard walls and the shell casing tittered as it bounced off the cement floor. Katherine staggered against the lockers, grabbed at the bench, and fell, scattering papers and pictures all around her. I stepped over and felt the vest under her coat.

"I thought you'd wear a vest. Figured it had to be a head shot."

She had both hands pressed to her leg and bit against the pain. Then she looked up and shook her head.

"You still don't have the stomach, Michael. You never did."

I pressed the gun to her temple and let her rethink things. Then I raised the butt and cracked her once along the side of the skull. She fell back against the wall, unconscious. I checked her pulse, then her leg. She'd live. I pulled out her cuffs and shackled her to a locker door. Then I pocketed her cell phone, collected the paperwork I'd brought on CMT, and left the subway.

Katherine Lawson could not have been more wrong. It was easy to pull the trigger. Too much so. The courage lay in putting the gun back in my pocket and walking away.

CHAPTER 57

A solitary figure stepped out of the black and walked along the tracks, a thin pistol in his right hand. There was no sound, save his own languid footsteps and the rats, scratching against the darkness. The man moved closer to the wall and stopped. He'd tracked the woman here, then waited. He'd heard the voices, but couldn't make out any words. Then, the gunshot. Maybe someone had done the man a favor. Now he'd find out.

Just ahead, he saw a shallow pool of white floating against the black. The man crept closer and clicked on his flashlight. She was crumpled in a corner, eyes closed, breathing even. Her left hand was cuffed to a locker, and she'd taken a bullet in the leg. The man crouched down to take a closer look. Flesh wound. Hardly this woman's biggest problem. He glanced at the scatter of paperwork on the floor, but didn't bother with any of it. He hadn't been told to read anything. Hadn't been told to collect anything. And the man did what he was told. He compared the woman's face with the picture they'd given him. Then he stood up, raised his pistol, and fired twice. Two tiny pops. Two small holes.

THE THIRD RAIL

He checked the woman again. Satisfied, the man slipped the pistol into his coat and pulled the gray cashmere close around him. Then he turned and walked away, his left foot dragging behind him. The man hated rats and could feel them as he walked, staring out at him from the darkness.

CHAPTER 58

The call came at eight the next morning. I was up on Rachel's floor by eight-fifteen. Hazel was not there to greet me. Instead, it was a sad-eyed doctor named John Sokul. He slid a summary of Rachel's injuries in front of me.

"Just so you know what we've been dealing with, Mr. Kelly."

I scanned the sheet. A fractured skull, two cracked ribs, fractured collarbone, fingers, and cheek.

"As you know, there were two assailants," the doctor said. "According to Rachel, they hit her with a brick so she was at least partially unconscious during the attack. There was no sexual assault, but, of course, this was a brutal attack. We've kept her under mild sedation due to the extensive physical injuries, but also to ease the mental and emotional trauma she's suffered."

"And now?"

"And now she needs to reenter the world. Or at least start the process. She's been mostly withdrawn, which is not unusual. She answers our questions and takes all her medication, but she doesn't offer anything on her own. She doesn't react well to most physical contact and typically will not allow any male member of our staff to touch her at all."

"What does she do all day?"

"Most of the time, she just sits in our common room and looks out the window. And she holds that dog you brought, Maggie. She holds that dog all day."

RACHEL WAS SITTING with her back to the door, by a window overlooking the lake. She had a splint on one hand and the pup cradled in both arms. I approached quietly. She turned as I sat down beside her. One side of her face was swollen with bruises, and her left eye was still partially shut. There were stitches holding together her lower lip, and one cheek was covered by a bandage. Maggie wagged her tail and squirmed in Rachel's arms. She let the pup go, and I picked her up. The pup licked my face.

"She misses you."

"Yeah." I put the dog down. She scrambled across to Rachel, who gathered her up again.

"How you doing?" I said.

Rachel scratched the dog's ears and turned back to the lake. "My face hurts. I feel like I'm about a hundred and I got viciously attacked by some fucking animals. That doesn't include the quality time I spent with your friend Jim."

I reached out to touch her sleeve.

"Don't." I thought she might push me away, but she just hugged the pup, who buried her head under Rachel's arm.

"You know all the work I do with the Rape Volunteer Association?" she said.

The association was a support group for women who'd been assaulted. I'd met Rachel at its annual fund-raiser.

"Sure."

"I used to think I shared this special bond with the victims. Felt their pain just because I felt something. Truth is, I was clueless, smiling like an idiot, trying to comfort someone about something I knew absolutely nothing about."

"You think the women you helped feel that way?"

"If I were them, I would."

I shook my head and joined her in looking out the window. After ten minutes or so, Rachel sighed. I ran my fingertips across her hand. She dropped her head to my shoulder, and I slipped an arm around her. She felt thin and brittle. The pup yawned and wagged her tail slowly.

"I'm sorry, Rach."

"I know." Her face was wet and I brushed away a tear. She swore and dabbed at her face with the back of her sleeve. "Pretty bad when you're no longer aware you're crying."

"It'll get better, babe."

"Maybe, but it won't be the same."

We fell back into the chasm of silence. After a while, Rachel moved to a chair across from me and leaned forward.

"I don't know where anything goes from here," she said.

"We'll figure it out, Rach. Day at a time."

She held up a finger, close to my lips, but not touching. "Shh, Michael. Listen."

I fell quiet.

"It's not always about figuring," she said. "And it's not always about 'we.' "

I felt the cold touch my heart, the lovely bruise rising with her name on it, the ache I was already pretending wasn't there.

"That's all right," I said, smiling hard against the lie.

"No, it's not, Michael. But sometimes things happen. And sometimes there's no going back. The truth is, we just don't fit in each other's lives. No matter how hard I try to convince myself otherwise."

I stared at a cracked tile on the floor. She tilted my chin up until my eyes met hers. Then she took my hand, kissed it and laid it against her cheek. That was when I felt her pity and knew it was real. And that was probably the worst thing of all.

We sat that way for another minute or so. Then the doctor stepped in from the corridor and gave me the sign to wrap it up.

"I think they're booting me out of here," I said. Rachel tried to stand and winced.

"Careful," I said.

"I know. Whole fucking thing's falling apart on me."

I smiled. She laughed, and that led to another spate of crying that finally subsided.

"Will you stop by again?" she said.

"That what you want?" My voice felt dry and tight.

"A visit would be nice, yes."

Maggie jumped up and crawled close. Rachel gathered the pup into her lap. "All right if I keep her for a while?"

"Sure."

Rachel traced a finger across the back of my hand. "Thanks for coming."

"Thanks for letting me in."

She nodded and seemed suddenly tired, suddenly adrift. I tried to keep her close, but she rolled away from me like the tide, leaving nothing between us but a bare beach, littered with the bones of a broken relationship.

I kissed her carefully and gave the pup's ears a scratch. Then I left. Rachel turned back to her view of the lake. Maggie's eyes followed me all the way to the door.

CHAPTER 59

Rodriguez was sitting in a no-parking zone, sunglasses on, engine running. I slid into the passenger's side. "How'd it go?" he said.

"About what you'd expect."

The detective nodded and took a look in his rearview mirror. Then he wheeled away from the curb. "I've been up to see her a couple of times."

"Her nurse told me. Told me it was a big help."

"I know a little bit about this. From Nicole and everything."

"I remember."

Rodriguez sighed. "If you got a problem . . ." He glanced across the car.

"It's okay, Vince. Anything you can do to make her better. I appreciate it."

We drove for a while in silence. Rodriguez turned on the radio, then snapped it off. "You okay to talk a little shop?"

I looked over. "Sure."

"Wilson called me in this morning."

"How is the mayor?"

"Happy as the proverbial pig in shit. He told me about your train crash. About Transco and CMT Holding."

"Probably figured I'd fill you in anyway. What do you think?"

"I think our mayor owns the cardinal, lock, stock, and altar boys."

"Nice to keep the mayor happy," I said. "By the way, what ever happened with Alvarez?"

Rita Alvarez had gotten her exclusive. Scooped both Chicago dailies on the scene inside Cabrini and was promised an "inside look" at the task force that hunted down and killed Jim Doherty.

"Funny you should ask." Rodriguez smiled lightly.

"Date tonight?"

"Dinner at the Chop House."

I leaned back in my seat and thought about my friend and the reporter. Maybe not such a bad thing.

Rodriguez hit his blinker, took a left, and pulled up to a red light at the corner of LaSalle and Chicago. "There was something else that came up."

A young woman was screaming at a young man at a bus stop. The man grabbed the woman's arm. She shook him off and stalked away.

"What's that?" I said.

The man started to follow the woman across Chicago Avenue and almost got hit by a bus. He stepped back onto the curb, then found a bench and lit a cigarette.

"Dispatch took an anonymous call last night. A woman shot down in the subway."

"Hadn't heard about that," I said.

"You won't. It was Katherine Lawson. They traced the call

to her cell phone. Found her body down by the tracks where Maria Jackson was found."

I felt my head snap around. "Her body?"

Rodriguez nodded and hit the gas as the light turned. "Shot three times with two different guns. A thirty-eight in the leg and a couple of twenty-two slugs to the head."

"Strange."

"Yeah. By the way, you still got that cold thirty-eight I gave you before Cabrini?"

I could feel the heavy gaze of the homicide cop walk its way across the car.

"Probably not," I said.

Rodriguez grunted and we drove a little more.

"When you talked to the mayor this morning," I said, "did he tell you about Lawson?"

The detective looked over again. "You mean how she was shaking down the church?"

I nodded.

"Yeah, he mentioned it. When did you turn up that part of it?"

"Just the last day or so. I would have told you, but . . ." I shrugged.

"Some things I'm better off not knowing."

"Probably. You gonna pull her case?"

Rodriguez shook his head. "Feds usually handle it when one of their own dies."

"Which means what?"

"Lawson was dirty. If it was Chicago PD, the whole thing would get buried. My guess is the Bureau's no different. We're holding the evidence, but I'm betting it never gets touched."

"So we're done with that?"

"Looks that way." The detective tapped two fingers lightly against the steering wheel. "Where you headed?"

"Home."

"Good idea." Rodriguez turned up the radio and steered his car toward Lake Shore Drive. I didn't say another word.

CHAPTER 60

I woke to the quiet of midafternoon, thinking about Katherine Lawson. I'd left her alive in the subway. Then someone came along and decided to finish the job. I wondered who. Better yet, why.

I sat up on my couch and considered the fat canvas bag on my coffee table. I'd told the mayor's accountant, Walter Sopak, part of Lawson's story. The part about Lawson's little girl. Sopak and his laptop agreed to meet me at an all-night Mexican place called El Presidente on Wrightwood and Ashland. A couple bowls of chili and a chimichanga later, the accountant had cracked Lawson's computer and emptied one of her offshore bank accounts. The bag was stuffed with Sopak's good deeds—three-quarters of a million dollars the feds would never miss. I had an appointment with a trust officer at Chase set up for tomorrow morning. The account would be in the name of Melanie Lawson. She'd be informed of the money when she hit twenty and be able to access it a year later. The trust officer at Chase figured the account would be worth almost two million by then. I wasn't entirely convinced Chase would still be in business, never mind turning anyone a profit, but what was a guy to do. So we'd all take a chance.

I walked over to my desk and locked the money in a drawer. From a second drawer, I took out the whiskey, along with some pieces from the past. The first photo was a parting glass, my dad laid out in his only suit, waiting for them to fire up the funeral home's oven and send him into eternity. My old man's face had shrunk in death, collapsed into the empty shell that was his life. The red eyes I knew as a nine-year-old were thankfully sewn shut. The fists that broke my mom's jaw in five places were gone as well, replaced by a pair of pale hands clutching a set of rosary beads for all they were worth. I toasted the old man with a bit of Macallan. Good luck with that.

The second shot I pulled was of Hubert Russell, moments after they'd cut him down. The rope was still twisted around his neck, and there was a small tattoo, a yellow star, on the side of his throat. I remembered it from the first time I met him, minding his own business at the Cook County Bureau of Land Records, thinking his life was just beginning.

I turned Hubert's picture facedown and walked myself and my glass over to the front windows. The sparrow was back, hopping back and forth on its branch, eyeing me with a distinct measure of disdain. I cracked the closest window, and the bird took off. I opened it some more and felt the bleak fingers of a winter sun on my face. I breathed deep, let the cold air chill my lungs, and thought about Rachel, wondered if my phone would ever ring. Then I looked down the street. The black car was there, same spot as yesterday. I had run the tag, wasn't surprised when it came back to the archdiocese. They seemed to enjoy watching me watch them. Or maybe they had nothing better to do.

I didn't know if the city's holy men were involved in Hubert's death. Every instinct told me no. So I believed. Guess that's why they call it faith. As for the blood on their hands from thirty years past, I'd leave that for Judgment Day and a higher authority. Until then, the men in collars would live under the thumb of Chicago's mayor. And that seemed purgatory enough for any man.

I shut the window and finished my drink. Then I found my coat and headed for the door. The weather had softened and the streets in my neighborhood were crowded, blessedly so. I walked up and down them until, finally, I disappeared into the forgiving crush.

EPILOGUE

The evidence room sits in the basement of Area 4 on Chicago's West Side. Tucked up high on a shelf, about halfway down the length of the room, is a cardboard box sealed with evidence tape. Inside it are a sheaf of pages, dried and crusted with blood, found in the subway under Katherine Lawson's body.

No one ever gave the pages a close read. Everyone, it seems, had a reason not to. The federal government was too arrogant. The city of Chicago, too complacent. And Michael Kelly, too angry.

If anyone had taken a look, they would have first discovered the material Lawson had copied from the "Terror 2000" binder Jim Doherty had with him when he died. A reading of the highlighted passages would have revealed Doherty's focus on what the Pentagon called the "subway scenario": the introduction of lightbulbs filled with weaponized anthrax into a major urban subway system.

Anyone reading farther would have discovered Katherine Lawson's own notes, detailing the background of Jim Doherty's accomplice, Robert Robles, including his two-year stint at Fort Detrick in Maryland, as well as the lab's own experiments with weaponized anthrax. Finally, they would have found the article Lawson clipped from the *Baltimore Sun*, highlighting the lab's missing cache of bioweapons.

All of this could have been gleaned from Katherine Lawson's notes. If anyone had bothered to look. Instead, the whole troublesome problem was stuffed into an evidence box and buried. Meanwhile, a few miles away, along a run of track close to where Lawson's body was discovered, two lightbulbs rattled and hummed in their sockets, growing looser by the day and with the rumble of every passing CTA train. No one could predict when one or both bulbs would fall. No one knew for sure what was inside. Or what wasn't. Like most everything else, it was mostly a flick of the wrist, a roll of the dice. And the courage to live with the consequences.

AUTHOR'S NOTE

On February 4, 1977, four CTA cars came off the rails of Chicago's L and crashed into the street at the corner of Lake and Wabash in Chicago's Loop. Eleven people were killed and picture of L trains hanging off the tracks were splashed across page one in newspapers across the country. The cause of the accident was eventually determined to be operator error. For a good account of the accident, check out the *Chicago Tribune's* next-day story at **http://chicago-l.org/articles/1977crash1.html**. You might notice that one of the article's authors is a young reporter named David Axelrod, architect of Barack Obama's run for the White House and now a senior adviser to the president.

For those of you interested in the security of U.S. bio-research facilities, work at the largest such lab at Fort Detrick, in Maryland, was suspended in early 2009 because of concerns about the lab's inventory of pathogen samples. For more information, see **www.washingtonpost.com/wp-dyn/.../AR2009020903511. html**. More than 9,000 unaccounted-for samples turned up in various freezers and lockers at the facility, and a criminal investigation was ordered. See the story at **www.washingtonpost.**

com/wpdyn/.../AR2009061703271.html. For more information gen-
erally, Google "Fort Detrick disease samples."

"Terror 2000" was the name of an actual Pentagon report,
issued in 1993 and never released to the public because the
government deemed it too disturbing. Among the scenarios
reportedly contemplated: anthrax being released in a subway
and commercial airliners being flown into government buildings and the World Trade Center. See **http://old.911digitalarchive.
org/crr/documents/985.pdf**.

The problem of fraud and embezzlement in the Catholic
church, and specifically at the parish level, is a growing one.
For more information, you can check out these links: **http://
www.nytimes.com/2007/01/05/us/05church.html?_r=1** and **http://www.
catholic.org./national/national_story.php?id=22413**.

For those of you who might go looking for a Bucktown coffee shop named Filter, don't bother. It's gone, but not forgotten. For those of you who might find yourself on Southport
Avenue looking for an old, broken-down L station, again,
don't bother. The city just replaced it with a brand-new one.
And, finally, if you go to Chicago's Holy Name Cathedral for
the weekday 12:30 mass, it actually begins at 12:10.

ACKNOWLEDGMENTS

Thanks, first of all, to everyone who has bought and read *The Chicago Way* and *The Fifth Floor*. Hope you like this one.

Thanks to my editor, Jordan Pavlin, and to all the folks at Knopf and Vintage/Black Lizard who have provided me with such amazing support. Special thanks to Laura Baratto, Sue Betz, Jason Booher, Bridget Fitzgerald, Erinn Hartman, Jim Kimball, Leslie Levine, Jennifer Marshall, Maria Massey, Claire Bradley Ong, Russell Perreault, Zach Wagman, and Iris Weinstein.

Thanks to David Gernert for being such a great agent and friend. Thanks to Chicago writer Garnett Kilberg Cohen, who also teaches at Columbia College, Chicago, for plowing through a first draft and zeroing in on what was working and, especially, what wasn't.

Thanks to my family and friends for their love and encouragement. A special shout-out to Mal Flanagan. Get better, pal.

Finally, I'd like to remember Jake O'Donnell. I was lucky enough to call him a friend. We miss you, Jake.

That's it. Love you, Mary Frances.

A NOTE ABOUT THE AUTHOR

Michael Harvey is the author of two other Michael Kelly books, *The Chicago Way* and *The Fifth Floor*, as well as a journalist and documentary producer. His work has won numerous national and international awards, including multiple Emmy Awards and an Academy Award nomination. Mr. Harvey earned a law degree from Duke University, a master's degree in journalism from Northwestern University, and a bachelor's degree in classical languages from Holy Cross College. Additional information can be found at www.michaelharveybooks.com.

A NOTE ON THE TYPE

The text of this book was composed in Trump Mediæval.
Designed by Professor Georg Trump (1896–1985) in the mid-1950s,
Trump Mediæval was cut and cast by the C. E. Weber Type Foundry
of Stuttgart, Germany. The roman letter forms are based on classical
prototypes, but Professor Trump has imbued them with his own un-
mistakable style. The italic letter forms, unlike those of so many
other typefaces, are closely related to their roman counterparts.